New Series ROMANTIC COMEDY

"So, like, when's the wedding?"

Holden's teenaged stepbrother asked between bites of beef jerky. "And aren't you supposed to be all sappy? I mean, like, you just got engaged. And where's the ring? Dad gave his last fiancée a three-carat diamond ring she could use as a paperweight. It's not like you to be a cheapskate, Holden. Right now my sister's talking wedding gowns with Taylor. Sis thinks a flesh-colored, skintight leather leotard under a big white net cage would be cool—but you didn't even give Taylor a ring yet."

"There isn't going to be a—" Holden shut his mouth. A secret wasn't safe in this full house. *A ring.* Holden hadn't even thought about a ring. He'd been too busy thinking about how to get Taylor back into his arms without leading her to think this mock engagement might actually have a future....

Dear Reader,

Welcome to another month of LOVE & LAUGHTER, a look at the lighter side of love. Taking our inspiration from the beloved screwball comedies of yesterday to the romantic comedies of today, we searched high and low, far and wide, just about everywhere, in fact, for authors who love and write romance and comedy. The results, if we dare be so immodest, have been absolutely fabulous.

This month *New York Times* bestselling author Kasey Michaels, known both for her romance fiction from Silhouette and mainstream historical romance novels, delights with *Five's a Crowd*. Her comic tale of lovers who never get to be alone is warm and emotional and funny. We are thrilled to have Kasey in the LOVE & LAUGHTER lineup.

RITA Award-winning Jennifer Crusie simply continues to amaze us with her talent. She has very quickly become a reader favorite, and *Anyone But You* will win her many more fans. Her heroine, Nina, was beginning her life fresh—new job, new apartment. No husband. All she wanted was a puppy. A happy, perky puppy. Instead she got Fred. Part basset, part beagle, part manic-depressive…and things only get crazier from there.

With love—and laughter,

Malle Vallik

Malle Vallik
Associate Senior Editor

FIVE'S A CROWD
Kasey Michaels

Harlequin Books

TORONTO • NEW YORK • LONDON
AMSTERDAM • PARIS • SYDNEY • HAMBURG
STOCKHOLM • ATHENS • TOKYO • MILAN
MADRID • WARSAW • BUDAPEST • AUCKLAND

ISBN 0-373-44003-0

FIVE'S A CROWD

Kasey Michaels is a *New York Times* bestselling author who is closing in on the writing of her fiftieth book (saying she lost count somewhere in the mid-forties—and not mentioning whether she means the number of books or her age). In addition to writing over a dozen books for Silhouette, she has penned many mainstream historical novels that have garnered her both a Romance Writers of America RITA award and a *Romantic Times* award. Ms. Michaels greatly enjoys writing for Love & Laughter, as she is a firm believer that the highway to true love always includes more than a few easily-laughed-away potholes!

Don't miss Kasey's short story in *A Funny Thing Happened on the Way to the Delivery Room,* on sale from Silhouette for Mother's Day, 1997!

To massage therapist Krisann Albanese,
a true "hands-on" buddy!
Sorry about the bird....

And to Doctor Joseph and Darlene Stella.
Friends when friends were needed!

1

MASTERS SACKED BY CHEVY, DISAPPEARS
byline Rich "The Nose" Newsome

Holden Masters, Philadelphia's scrambling, five-time All-Pro Quarterback, who has eluded serious injury for all of his eleven seasons in the NFL, was allegedly blindsided on I-95 by a drunk in a 1988 Chevrolet while on his way home from a banquet in his honor two nights ago, this reporter has just learned.

Although Masters's familiar cherry red Ferrari was totaled in the accident, his injuries, says his agent, Sidney Feldon, are minor. University of Pennsylvania doctors agree that Masters did not require hospitalization, but both the extent of his injuries and his whereabouts since being treated in the Emergency Room are already a closely guarded secret, even from the team's management.

With contract negotiations for the eight-million-dollar grid star promised to begin in earnest shortly, and hopes for a return to the

Super Bowl running high in the City of Brotherly Love, Feldon assured the media at a hastily gathered predawn press conference that Masters will be one hundred percent for the fall season.

If this is so, this reporter has a few questions. Why did it take two days and a leak to the press to learn of Masters's injury? Where is Holden Masters now, and why is he only speaking through his agent?

Well, Masters? Do you have any answers for us, because we'd sure like to hear them?

"THAT MISERABLE, no good son of a—Sid, this is all your fault!" The newspaper was thrown to the floor, then stomped on. It would have been much more satisfying to take Rich "The Nose" Newsome's miserable rag, crush it in his hands and slam-dunk it into the nearest waste can.

But Holden Masters wasn't up to crushing anything, even a newspaper. Not with his right arm, his *throwing* arm, his most powerful offensive weapon, in a sling.

"Holden, you're throwing a hissy fit, if I might point out the obvious," Sidney Feldon observed from his lounging position on Masters's soft white leather couch. He crossed his legs, attempting to appear at ease, which wasn't easy—not with the star client pacing the carpet, steam pouring out his ears. "It's unbecoming in the MVP of last year's Super Bowl.

Mickey Mouse, for one, would not approve. Now, sit down like a good little quarterback, and I'll tell you what I've done.''

Holden shot his agent a look that would have most rational, self-protective persons scurrying for safety behind a potted plant and began pacing the Oriental carpet that had been a gift from his jet-setting mother. "I already know what you've done, Sid," he flung at the agent, wishing the man would abandon the toupee he had begun wearing only a few months previously. He looked like he had a dead rat on his head.

"I've put your name on the lips of every team owner in the NFL," Sid said, openly preening.

"Wrong! You've taken a lousy molehill and built it into a freaking mountain! Look at me, will you? Not a break, Sid, not even a sprain. A *wrench!* Isn't that what the doctor said? A *wrench!* A little rest, a little rehab, and I'll be good as new. I don't even need this miserable sling."

And to prove his point, Holden lifted his right arm away from his body, ready to slide the sling up and over his head. "Damn!" he exploded, grabbing his shoulder as the pain sliced through him, weakening his knees. He sat down before he fell down.

"Bruises, contusions and a soft-tissue injury to the—what was that called, Holden? Some Latin word, right?" Sid asked, uncrossing his legs as he took another sip of orange juice. "Well, whatever. It certainly looks painful enough. And delightfully colorful. What's more important, the docs say it will be six to eight weeks until you're back to your full strength. And that's if you behave yourself. You're not especially *good* at behaving yourself, Holden, do you know that?''

Holden glared at the man. ''I don't know, Sid. I haven't strangled you yet, have I?''

''Good point,'' Sid answered briskly, rising to his feet and going over to the small refrigerator built into the wet bar to refill his glass.

He then put the glass, and his elbows, on the bar, and sighed theatrically as he looked at his best client, his good friend and the man whose talent had already assured Sid of a financially comfortable old age.

Holden Masters was an agent's dream. Not only was he possibly the best quarterback to come along in this century, he was a handsome devil and marketable in a million ways. In his prime at thirty-two, Holden was six-four without his cleats, with a broad-shouldered, slim-hipped, athletically perfect body beneath his tight-fitting maroon-and-gold uniform.

Black hair, green eyes, a killer smile…oh, yeah, the man was the darling of Madison Avenue, the idol of every young kid with dreams of playing pro ball one day, the icon of every middle-aged man with a gut and a mortgage, and the heartthrob of every female in America old enough to put away her Barbie dolls and young enough to enjoy visions of having the Master of the Game alone in the sack with her.

He was, in a word, a living license to print money, and Sidney Feldon could smell a buck from a mile away. Not that he didn't honestly, truly, like Holden. Everybody liked Holden. He was that kind of guy. He took chances on the football field, never taking the easy way into a slide when he could leap over defenders and into the end zone. He meant excitement on and off the field, living the good life, driving fast cars, loving 'em and leaving 'em on a routine basis.

In fact, if Sidney could be anyone in the world, he'd be Holden Masters. Who wouldn't?

"Holden," Sid said now, "you're a schmuck."

"I'm a *what?*" Holden asked, swiveling in his seat, the better to glare at his friend and agent.

"A schmuck. A stupid, dumb schmuck," Sid returned affably, still leaning on the bar. "Don't you see what we've got here? We have the press and the public by the throat, that's what we've got. We've got the owners sweating bullets. We've got a contract ready to be signed, making you the highest paid player in history. And all you have to do is disappear for the next eight weeks. Disappear, do your therapy and show up the first day of negotiations with your arm and shoulder one hundred percent. The owners are tearing their hair out, thinking you're all but dead, or worse. I'll get another two mil out of them the minute you show up on the practice field and rifle that ball a quick seventy yards.''

"That's nuts, Sid.''

"That's show biz, Holden," the agent answered, lifting his glass to toast his own brilliance. "Now, down to brass tacks," he said, coming around to the front of the bar and perching his chubby, five-foot-four frame on one of the bar stools. "I've arranged for a physical therapist to meet you at a little hideaway where you can do your rehab undisturbed.''

"A physical therapist? Who?''

"Relax. Taylor's both a physical therapist and a massage therapist—like getting two for the price of one. Registered, has all the right papers—like a pedigree dog, but with real talent, you understand? You stay at the hideaway, out of sight of the press, most especially out of sight of The Nose, and do your thing. Oh—and you'll have to shave that mustache. Seeing as how you've had it since college, nobody will know you without it. Meantime, I'm off to Maui, where The Nose won't find me, either. Secrecy, Holden. That's the key. That's what's going to bring in all those lovely dollars.''

Holden eyed his agent warily as he stroked his mustache, already missing it. "Hideaway? What hideaway? Where? Remember, I promised Peter I'd take Woody for the summer. No twenty-three-year-old kid is going to be happy stuck away in some cabin in the middle of nowhere, you know. And Tiffany's been making noises about joining us, God help me. And what about Amanda?''

Holden shook his head. "Never mind that last part. I've been trying to convince Amanda that we're just friends—not that she's taking the hint. I think she's seeing dollar signs and wedding rings, which were never a part of our bargain. If you're putting me in the middle of nowhere for eight weeks, she'll be bored out of her skull and maybe go away. In fact, they might *all* go away.''

"There is that, yes,'' Sid said, sensing that he had won the first battle. "Amanda's time is definitely up. And no, your lovely supermodel flavor of the month won't like this place one bit.''

Holden looked at Sid, smiling. "Keep talking, old friend. I think I'm beginning to like this. Where are you sending me?''

"New Jersey,'' Sid answered cheerfully, then belatedly gave in to a moment of self-preserving sanity and ducked back behind the bar.

"New Jersey? Who in their right mind goes to...?'' Holden grinned. "Perfect, Sid. Perfect. Nobody will think to look for me there. Not even my own mother. Hell, *especially* my own mother! She only recognizes three states—New York, Florida and California. Plus Nevada, of course. Best little divorce state in the world, or so she says, and she ought to know.''

Sid sagged against the bar, knowing the worst was over. Holden had agreed. He rushed into speech.

"You'll love it, Holden. I used to go to New Jersey as a kid—got me out of Manhattan in the summertime, you know? I rented you a condo in Ocean City, a nice, family-type resort town where you'll be able to rest and do your rehab, and Woody and Tiffany can loll on the beach and work on their tans. It isn't California, but sand is sand, right? I've even hired a housekeeper. It's perfect, Holden. Perfect!"

"It's New Jersey, Sid," Holden responded dully, rubbing his sore, stiff shoulder as he thought about the next eight weeks. "Don't go nuts."

TAYLOR ANGEL LOOKED at the paper in her hand, then peered out the window of her car at the building in front of her. *Yup,* she told herself rather smugly, *this must be the place. And only three wrong turns and a quarter hour of backtracking. None too shabby, Taylor, old girl, none too shabby.*

"Parking in the rear, the man said," she mumbled as she put the car in gear and drove to the corner, turning right and locating the narrow alley behind the house or "condo" as the real-estate agent who'd handed her the key called the place. Ugly, that's how Taylor would have described it, pulling onto the wide concrete drive behind the condo and looking up at the pale green stucco walls. Lime green. Baby-mess-in-the-diaper green. Tutti-fruti-rooti ice sherbet green. But festive, she supposed, feeling charitable.

She popped the back doors of her two-year-old minivan and pulled out three large canvas bags containing her personal belongings, then closed the doors again on her massage table and other professional gear, figuring she had plenty of time to set up her stuff once she'd picked a good area to convert to a workout room. For now, she just wanted to get inside, get herself settled and take a run on the beach before sundown.

Juggling the bags and the key, she walked to the entrance of the condo, which was on the side of the long building, noticed that the door was already unlocked, then checked the address once more, just to be sure. There were two of these huge, homely green buildings, each divided into two side-by-side condos, and she didn't want to go tripping into the wrong one.

She shook her head, mentally berating herself for having such a negative attitude. The condo wasn't all *that* ugly, for one thing. So it was an unfortunate color. So what? From the looks of the outside of it, the place was massive, with several decks at both ends and a flat roof that probably would be a great place to sit and watch the ocean, which was only a block away.

She had been promised her own room and private bath. A housekeeper would take care of meals. All she had to do was whip Holden Masters back into shape and she was outta there—along with having a good rest, getting a killer tan, and waking to the sound of surf for the next eight weeks. Not exactly a sentence of two months at hard labor.

And—with the lovely bonus Sidney Feldon had already given her—not too shabby in the financial department, either.

Taylor pushed the open door a little more ajar and called out; "Hello? anybody home?"

There was no answer. Knowing she was in the right place, she shrugged and walked in and immediately felt the coolness of central air-conditioning that was several degrees lower than the late-morning June heat outside.

Putting down her bags, she decided the first thing she'd do would be to scope out the place, rather like a child playing house. She walked across the tile foyer in the center of the condo and laid a hand on the white pipe railing, looking straight up past miles and miles of curving white pipe, all the way to the ceiling that was—she counted quickly—about four levels up.

"Good exercise for the client," she said, walking to the front of the condo and the large, neatly furnished living room with wet bar. Sliding glass doors, three pair of them, looked out over a small, ground-level patio, and there was both a television set and a VCR in a cabinet in the corner.

"Perfect for my table," she announced to the room, then retraced her steps past the foyer and down a long hall to open the doors that lined it.

The first held the heating and air-conditioning unit, the second a large bathroom, and the third led to what she immediately claimed as her bedroom. Behind the bedroom was the garage and a dumbwaiter. Three bikes were lined up beside the dumbwaiter and she itched to pull one out and take it for a spin.

But first things first! She took her canvas bags to the bedroom and threw them on the bed, then went off to climb the stairs—feeling like Jack shinnying his way up the beanstalk—to the next level.

The half flight led to a hallway to the rear of the condo, and she found two bedrooms there, connected by a Jack-and-Jill bathroom, a small powder room in the hall, as well as a complete laundry room.

Another half flight took her to another living room at the front of the condo—and another television and VCR—also with sliding glass doors to yet another patio, one that provided a view of the ocean.

Up another half flight and she was in the rear of the condo again, this time facing a dining room, kitchen and what had to be the master suite, complete with separate bath and Jacuzzi. A sliding glass door in the dining room led to a full flight of stairs and the flat roof, generously littered with chairs and chaises and a spectacular view of Ocean City, the ocean and, she was fairly confident, the sight of the eight-miles-distant Atlantic City when night fell and the casino lights lit up the sky.

The homely green condo was, in a word, perfect! "Not exactly slumming, Taylor," she complimented herself as she skipped back down the stairs and let herself into the dining area once more—only to jump back out onto the landing and slide the door half-shut, narrowly avoiding being slammed in the gut by a half-pint, steely-eyed old lady wielding a broom like a baseball bat.

"Turn my back for a minute, and what happens?" the little old lady asked, clearly talking only to herself. "One of them football groupies sneaks in here, all blond hair and legs up to her neck, hoping to get lucky. Sam, dying was too good for you, leaving me alone like this, a defenseless old widow, made to fend for myself!"

Taylor took a deep breath, admonishing herself not to laugh, and opened the sliding glass door another half inch. "Mrs. Helper?" she called out tentatively. "You are Mrs. Helper, aren't you? The house-keeper? I'm Taylor Angel—Mr. Masters's therapist."

The old woman snorted, which had to be difficult to do, what with the lit cigarette dangling out of the corner of her Ida Lupino red lips. "Sure you are, honey. And I'm Miss America. Now, get out from behind that door and then get yourself out of my house. Therapist, my eye! And what sort of name is Taylor for a girl, I ask you?"

"A fairly miserable one, I admit," Taylor said, taking her life into her hands and stepping into the room, warily eying the broom. "But there's no nickname possible with Taylor, now is there? And using my initials wouldn't work, because I'm officially Taylor Noreen Angel, and that would make me T.N.A., and let me tell you, I have enough problems without that."

"T and A? Ha! I haven't heard that one since Sam gave up watching that there 'Charlie's Angels' show on the television!" The old woman dropped the broom and sat herself down at the dining-room table, laughing so hard tears squeezed out from under her heavily mascara-caked eyelashes. "Oh, sit down, girl," she commanded at last, indicating the chair across from her. "I don't bite. Bark a lot, but don't bite."

As soon as Taylor was seated, Mrs. Helper hopped up and went into the kitchen, talking as she went. "You'll have some iced tea with me, and then we'll sort things out, all right? Too damn many steps in this house, don't you think? I mean, what's an old woman to do—lugging groceries, dragging laundry. Eight weeks of this, and I'll be joining Sam—not that he wants me. Probably has himself two or three good-looking angels all to himself."

She came back into the room, carrying two glasses she then plunked down on the table. "There—you want sugar? Rot your teeth, sugar. But those substitutes are chock-full of chemicals that'll probably rot the rest of you. Drink it plain, honey. It'll put hair on your chest. Do you watch the soaps? I never miss my three o'clock show, so if any of you go asking for anything between three and four, you might as well ask the air. Don't budge an inch away from the set between three and four. Not in this lifetime anyway. That Masters fellow gets here first thing tomorrow, you know. Maybe you can lug the groceries up from my car. I'm parked right out front. You've got the legs for it, but I don't. Aren't you going to say anything, girl? Don't talk much, do you? My Sam was like that, yes, he was.''

''I can't imagine why,'' Taylor said, taking a sip of bitter tea and trying not to wince. ''And I'd be happy to help you, Mrs. Helper,'' she continued, unable to hide her wince anymore as she verbally tripped over ''help'' and ''Helper'' in the same tongue-twisting sentence. ''Did you know you could park your car out back? There's a dumbwaiter there, and that should make it easier to bring in the groceries.''

Mrs. Helper leaned forward, grinning around her cigarette. ''A dumbwaiter? You're kidding! So that's what those little doors are in every hallway, huh? Shoulda known. Sam and I went to a fancy hotel in the Catskills once, years ago. There was a dumbwaiter there, too. Sam got a little well-to-go one night—stinking drunk, you might say—and stuffed me into the dumbwaiter and sent me for a ride. I'm just a squirt, in case you haven't noticed, so I fit in just fine. Best fun I had in years. Want to try it? You can give me a boost up?''

Taylor's eyes watered as she choked on her bitter iced tea, trying to compose herself. "Another time, perhaps?'' she got out at last, rising from her chair and wondering if Ocean City was just another name for the rabbit hole in *Alice in Wonderland.*

"Whatever you say, Taylor,'' Mrs. Helper agreed cheerfully enough, picking up a huge bunch of keys on a chain decorated with several plastic disks advertising different brands of beer, and then following Taylor down the steps. "Let's just get cracking. I've got to get home and feed Killer.''

"Of course you do,'' Taylor answered, barely able to stay ahead of Mrs. Helper as the older woman sped down the stairs behind her. "Um . . . who is Killer?''

"My parakeet, of course. Used to have two of them. Called them Fred and George. Then . . . well, Fred is now Killer, if you take my meaning.''

"It's going to be a *long* summer, Ms. Angel, and you're going to earn every penny of that bonus,'' Taylor muttered under her breath as the housekeeper began telling her about the time she and her Sam had gone to a plumbers' convention in New York and dropped water balloons off the hotel roof.

2

HOLDEN MASTERS FELT naked without his mustache. But that was the least of his problems.

It had been a week since Sid had dropped his bombshell about the Ocean City condo, a long, boring week during which Holden had been able to lose the sling, but none of the stiffness in his shoulder and back, although his bruises had faded from deep purple to a pretty disgusting-looking orange-and-yellow mix.

He'd hidden out in his Philadelphia condo, his phone disconnected, ignoring the ringing doorbell and successfully dodging Rich "The Nose" Newsome this morning as he'd been snuck out the back door of his building in, of all things, a laundry cart. Just like in the movies—although in the movies, Holden was pretty sure, the star was smuggled out with the *clean* laundry.

He was even driving himself to Ocean City in a nondescript dark blue rental car—an automatic, as he couldn't use his right arm well enough for his favored five-on-the-floor stick shift.

After a week of hiding, he was more than ready for Sid's plan, eager for company, a little sunshine, maybe even a pair of dark sunglasses and a trip up the coast to one of the casinos. After all, pulling on those one-armed bandits could only be considered good therapy.

He saw the sign for the 7S exit off the Atlantic City Expressway and skillfully steered onto the ramp using only his left hand on the steering wheel, easing his foot off the gas as he came up against two lanes of bumper-to-bumper shore traffic and bade a wistful farewell to the speed he loved so well.

As he sat in his car going nowhere, he mentally traveled back to what really bothered him—and to the near future, which would probably quickly drive him out of his mind.

If only he had never given Woody his private number, and Woody hadn't passed it along to his younger sister, Tiffany. Then, all things considered, Holden wouldn't have believed the next eight weeks to be too bad.

But Tiffany had called. And, after fifteen minutes of abject pleading mingled with a few threats (a few of them from her father, who had grabbed the phone out of her hand), Tiffany was now coming to Ocean City. Tiffany and Woodstock LeGrand, his stepsiblings. The two of them. Together. In Holden's house. Under Holden's feet. Holden's responsibility.

It sounded like the cast and plot for a Grade-B horror movie.

He drummed his fingertips on the steering wheel as he thought about his odd, but strangely lovable family.

His mother, Miranda Masters LeGrand Higgins Tuques, was off touring some Greek islands with her fourth husband, Harry Tuques, self-proclaimed king of Pre-Cut Carpet, Inc., so at least he didn't have to worry about her swooping down on him with maternal tongue-cluckings and her three damn poodles in tow.

Holden smiled, shaking his head as he thought about his mother. Dear, sweet, lovely, flighty Miranda, who had too much money, too little sense and a firm belief that, to go to bed with her, a man must first make a detour to the nearest wedding chapel.

Which is how Holden had ended up with Woodstock and Tiffany LeGrand, two of Peter LeGrand's children, both from different marriages Peter had squeezed in before Miranda, who had been his third wife in a string of five? six? total trips to the altar.

Marriage. The bane of the world. The dumbest sort of bondage. Brief, disposable, but damned expensive if you did it in a community property state— which is why Miranda unfailingly did her divorcing in Nevada and her marrying in California.

She'd done all right with Holden's late father, the tennis-shoe magnate, but she'd hit the jackpot with her slightly reversed May-December marriage to Peter LeGrand, who'd first shown up on the pop charts in his teens and was still one of the acknowledged megastars of rock and roll. In fact, he was going out on tour with his band again this summer, which was one reason Woodstock, better known as Woody and just graduated from college, was coming east to stay with his big brother.

Tiffany was coming along because she was eighteen now, which made her only sixteen months younger than Peter's latest gum-popping bride—an awkward situation, to put it mildly.

When you got right down to it, both kids were too old to look good alongside their father, who was fifty-three now, but still trying to maintain his image as a sex magnet on tour. Way too old. But, unfortunately, not too old, or even close to too mature, to need a baby-sitter while Daddy Peter was away, smashing guitars on stage.

Holden forgot about his stepsiblings as traffic thinned out as he crossed the Ninth Street bridge into Ocean City and began looking for the turnoff to the condo Sid had rented for the summer.

Well, at least he didn't have to deal with Amanda Price, his girlfriend of the past six or so months—ever since they'd shot a jeans commercial together in Barbados. Amanda was a beautiful woman, a top-ranked supermodel, who looked great on his arm when he was out and about. Yes, a lovely woman. Ambitious. Maybe even driven. But without a lot of humor. And she'd been making noises about marriage lately, which always sent Holden running for the nearest exit.

Miranda was marriage. Peter was marriage. Holden did not believe in marriage!

Holden slowed the car as he searched out the address of the condo, peering out the passenger window to make out house numbers displayed in everything from seashells pasted onto railings to hand-painted knotty pine signs that displayed house names like Wistful Hideaway or Pop-Pop and Nana's Nest.

His attention was caught by the official Indy pace car parked in front of one of the larger condos—or at least it was, until a jogger passing along the sidewalk in front of the impressive car pushed all coherent thought from his mind and he nearly ran into the curb as he quickly switched his gaze to the rearview mirror.

The sight of the jogger moving away from him was on a par with the recent vision of her coming toward him. He had, he decided, rarely before seen spandex put to such good use as it was in the hot pink shorts and halter top of the ponytailed, honey blond female just now turning the next corner and disappearing from view.

Holden considered circling the block, eager for another, better, look at the young woman, then decided against it. He was here for a rest, and to work. Playtime would have to come later, after his arm was completely healed—and after Woody and Tiffany were back in California driving Peter nuts, not him.

"This Puritan work ethic of yours is becoming pretty damn boring, Masters," he grumbled aloud as he pulled the car to the curb in front of a building that instantly, crazily, reminded him of his long-ago love of lime Popsicles.

Leaving his luggage locked in the trunk, he climbed out of the car, stretched his cramped muscles—wincing as he tried to raise his arms above his head—and made his way up the brick path that led to the door at the side of the condo.

And then, he thought, the gods smiled at him. Because, just as he was fitting his key into the lock, he caught a glimpse of hot pink spandex out of the corner of his eye, coming toward him from the back of the condo.

"Lost the mustache, huh?" the honey blonde said, not even breathing hard as she continued to jog in place. "Can't say as I blame you. I've often wondered about that thing, you know. I mean, didn't it ever get caught on your face mask?"

There was no possible response to such a question, so Holden ignored it, although he did look at the young woman, deciding to give her the full benefit of the Masters smile. "Take a wrong turn, Pink Lady?"

She continued to jog in place, her own smile still pasted on her incredibly lovely, disturbingly intelligent face. "Nope. I'm your slave driver, Mr. Masters, here for the duration. Name's Angel. Taylor Angel. I got here yesterday. So, how *do* you feel about pain?"

Sid had sicced a female therapist on him? Was this his idea of a joke? If so, Holden wasn't laughing. He reached up to stroke his mustache with thumb and forefinger, then remembered that it was gone. "Depends on who is inflicting the pain, I suppose," he said without inflection, turning the key and pushing open the door. "Right now, I'd say I'm in favor of it—if my agent was within strangling distance. You coming in, or were you thinking of running a marathon before lunch?'

She shook her head. "Nope, no marathon. I already put in my two miles for the day. Just cooling down, you know," she said, then jogged past him into the condo, which gave him a mind-boggling vision of long legs, short shorts and games two interested people could play.

"Your room is on the top level," she told him before he could ask. "Mrs. Helper—Thelma—is upstairs, probably baking something sinfully fattening. There's a dumbwaiter in the garage if you can't carry your luggage yourself, although you should, as it would be good therapy. Not bad for a quarterback to keep his legs in shape, either. These stairs will come in handy on rainy days, so you don't have to miss a workout. You need more than bedroom eyes and a killer smile to play in the NFL, you know.''

Holden decided he hated Taylor Angel. Hated her a lot. Beautiful women were supposed to look great draped on his arm, but keep their mouths shut. This one might have the looks of a Christie Brinkley, but she had the mouth of a Joan Rivers, and he had to beat down an impulse to gag her with her own pony-tail.

''I'll remember that, Miss Angel,'' he said, not bothering to hide his sarcasm, ''if I decide to try batting my eyelashes at the defense before airing one out to Bill Evers in the end zone.''

The sarcasm floated right over her head, or she chose to ignore it. He was pretty sure it was the latter, for this woman wasn't the least bit dumb. ''Evers? Good man, though sometimes he looks like he's afraid of the ball. When he dropped that pass against Dallas in the play-offs last season, I nearly kicked in the television screen.''

Oh, good. She thought she knew football. Just what Holden didn't need. ''I never talk shop, Miss Angel,'' he told her as he went over to the staircase and looked up, all the way up, to the top floor. Why didn't Sid book him into a sixth-floor tenement? It probably would have had fewer stairs. ''I think I can smell brownies.''

"Thelma," Taylor reminded him, looking smug, most probably for his benefit. "Queen of the mix. If she can just add eggs and water, she's a gourmet baker. But she's a whiz with roast beef—just ask her. Come on," she added, turning for the door once more, "let's get your luggage. I want to see you on my table, so I can get an idea of how much work we have ahead of us."

See you on my table. The words stopped Holden in his tracks. "You're really a physical therapist? Why am I having trouble with this?"

"Physical therapist *and* licensed massage therapist, actually. You'll need more massage probably, according to what Sid told me about your injury," she responded as she walked outside, so that Holden had no choice except to follow her. "So Uncle Sid really didn't tell you about me? I wonder why."

"Uncle Sid?" *Oh, yeah. I'm going to kill that man.* "Sid's your uncle?"

She stood next to the trunk of the car, waiting for him to open it. "Courtesy uncle, actually. His parents and mine played bridge together eons ago, before his parents moved to Florida and mine to the boonies, as they call it. I was surprised when I got his call last week, but he said he wanted somebody he could trust not to go running to the tabloids with the story of your injury, either now or after my job is done. It made sense. Lots of people make money on you, don't they, Mr. Masters?"

"Dozens of them. And Sid makes most of it," Holden grumbled, opening the trunk and reaching in to pull out one of his suitcases, only to have Taylor reach out and grab his arm.

"Not that way, Mr. Masters," she admonished him, putting one hand on his forearm, the other on his back. Her pink spandex-encased body touched his from shoulder to hip, which did strange things to his concentration. "You're not using the correct muscles."

He ignored the ripple of awareness that cut through his body, concentrating on Taylor's words, rather than her hands, her slim body. Which wasn't easy. "What?"

"I'd give you the technical names for everything if I wanted to bore you out of your skull," she answered, "but it would be easier to say that you have injured your shoulder and, because it hurts when you do certain things—make certain moves—you have begun to overcompensate, using muscles that aren't injured to do what the injured ones used to do."

"You're kidding, right?"

"No, I'm not. And too much of that for too long a time, my friend, and you'll end up with lost muscle memory and a frozen shoulder, which also isn't a laughing matter. Now—stop shoving your elbow into your side to help yourself move and reach out with your whole arm to pick up the suitcase."

He did as she said. He didn't want to, hadn't even noticed that he had been moving incorrectly, but he wanted her to move away from him; move her honey blond hair and perfumed scent and strong hands far, far away from him.

Or closer.

"Damn!" he exclaimed as he fully extended his arm, then tried to lift the suitcase—sending a stabbing pain and a disturbing weakness through his right arm and shoulder. "That hurts."

"We'll fix it," Taylor said matter-of-factly, stepping in front of him and lifting out both suitcases at once, which made Holden long to fire her on the spot.

"*We*, Miss Angel?"

"Neither one of us can do it alone, Mr. Masters. I'll set up my table after lunch, and we can do a thorough evaluation then—take a few measurements, check your range of motion, that sort of stuff. Until then, you and Thelma can get acquainted," she flung back at him, then left him standing in the street.

"Will I see you at lunch?" he called after her, wishing he could have thought before he spoke. After all, it wasn't as if he'd miss her if she went away.

She turned and looked back at him. "I do plan to eat, yes. And this isn't some social experiment, Mr. Masters. This is my job and I plan to do it very, very well. You'll see me morning, noon and night for the next eight weeks. Get used to it!"

"I'll work on it," he snapped, then added, slamming down the trunk lid with his left hand, "and I'm still going to kill Sid."

TAYLOR HAD ALREADY thrown the suitcases on Holden's bed and was halfway down the seeming half-dozen small flights of stairs before he passed her going the other way. She smiled her most blighting smile and kept on going, not stopping until she was safely behind the closed door of her own bedroom.

"Uncle Sid—you're in big, *big* trouble!" she vowed, looking up at the ceiling, ordering her heart rate to slow to a reasonable speed. It had gone into overdrive the moment she'd laid eyes on Holden Masters and had actually skipped a beat when he'd smiled at her with those gorgeous green eyes. She wouldn't even think about what had happened to her when she'd touched him to correct his incorrect movement, when her fingers had pressed against the taut muscle beneath his black cotton-knit shirt.

"It's a job, Angel," she told herself as she left the room and entered the adjoining bathroom to splash cold water on her face. "Just another job."

She looked at herself in the mirror, pulled the band from her ponytail so that her hair fell to below her shoulders, and winced. "And in another hour, that *job* is going to be lying facedown and defenseless on your massage table while you put some Yanni on the CD player, oil up your hands and . . . oh, brother!"

She stripped off her jogging clothes and stepped into the shower, sticking her head beneath the needle-sharp spray, hoping to calm herself. It wasn't, after all, as if she hadn't given massages to a handsome, intelligent, famous, living Adonis of a man before this. There had been Geoff, right? Geoff, the golf pro. Geoff, who had become her first and only lover.

Bad comparison...

She rubbed shampoo into her hair. Maybe it wouldn't take eight weeks to get Holden Masters back into shape. He hadn't been injured all that long, hadn't had a lot of time to stiffen up or lose muscle memory. She could probably whip him into fighting strength in a couple of weeks. Three, tops. Three times a day for therapy, once a day for massage, some running on the beach to keep his general muscle tone and strengthen his legs—that shouldn't be bad. She could certainly handle that without going all sloppy or weak in the knees.

Yeah, right...

Three weeks of Holden Masters living in the same condo, with Thelma there for protection during the day and three floors of condo separating them the rest of the time, through all the long, long nights.

Three weeks of looking into those absurdly beautiful green eyes.

Three weeks of touching his body, of looking at him, stripped to the waist, lying on her massage table.

Three weeks of living closely, intimately, with the idol of millions, the face that had launched a thousand commercials, boosted the sales of a thousand products, the athlete who had just been named Star of the Millennium by some sports magazine.

Oh, yeah. She could do this.

Standing on her head.

Right.

"I'm in big trouble," Taylor groaned, turning the water to cold and sticking her head under the spray once more. "Big, *big* trouble!"

3

LUNCH HAD BEEN uneventful.

Well, "uneventful" was probably too tame a word, Holden thought as he rapidly made his way down to the lowest level of the condo. Nobody had died. That was a better description.

Thelma Helper had kept up a running commentary as she served fairly delicious tuna salad sandwiches, hard-boiled eggs, mounds of greasy potato chips and something resembling iced tea but "guaranteed to put hair on your chest—and maybe even your tongue"—all while telling Holden all about her Sam, who had wisely departed for Heaven some two decades earlier, probably just so he didn't have to listen to Thelma anymore.

Miss Taylor Angel had barely said a word, only nodding when he dared to suggest they not be so formal and call each other by their first names, and leaving the table before the dessert of chewy chocolate brownies arrived in order to prepare for his first "session." The way she had said the word, he fully expected to walk into the living room on the ground floor to find a rack, thumbscrews and, he was sure, an iron maiden named Angel.

What he found was a simple burgundy leather massage table set up in the middle of the room, complete with a doughnut-shaped extension pad at its head that he knew he would soon place his face on so that he could spend the next half hour or so helplessly staring at the floor while Taylor Angel tortured him.

But first, Holden Masters was going to have himself a little fun.

He walked into the room in his bare feet, all six feet four inches of him covered only by a small white towel he'd pulled from the bar in his bathroom and wrapped around his waist. He wasn't by nature a very vain man, but he knew his body was in prime condition and that he was not exactly repulsive to the female sex.

"Ready when you are, Taylor," he said, putting a hand to his waist, ready to strip off the towel as she looked up from the notebook she was writing in, then stared at him like a deer caught in headlights. "Where do you want me?"

"Siberia would be good," he thought he heard her say as she shut the notebook with an audible snap and rose to her feet. "I think we need some ground rules, Holden, old sport," she continued, patting the table, indicating that he should hop up on the six-foot-long surface she had covered with a towel.

"No biting, eye gouging, or holding and hitting in the clinches?" he suggested, feeling more vulnerable than threatening as she stood on the other side of the table and ran a finger down the length of his spine.

"Nice, straight spine. Yes, definitely no holding and hitting. That's good for starters, I suppose," she answered, walking around to stand in front of him as his legs dangled several inches above the floor. "But I was thinking more of a dress code. I'll be working on your upper body, Holden, not your—"

"Gluteus maximus?" Holden offered, and had to smother a smile as he watched color rush into Taylor's face.

"Pompous ass was more what I was searching for," she countered, taking hold of his forearm. "Hop down, please. I want to measure your range of motion. Then we'll get started."

A half hour, several measurements and considerable pain later—although Holden refused to mutter a single curse as Taylor lifted his arm above his head, then clucked her tongue at his impeded movement— he was facedown on the table, staring at the carpet just as he'd supposed.

Soft, rather comforting piano music drifted from the portable CD player Taylor had turned on, and he reached down to his waist and pulled the towel away, revealing the team shorts he was wearing beneath them.

"Stupid human trick, Taylor. I'm sorry," he mumbled in apology, then flinched as she placed soft, yet strong hands on his upper shoulders and began what he would later term as fifteen minutes of hell followed by an equal quarter hour of heaven.

He'd never been injured before, not even in high school or college. He'd never had more than a few transitory muscle aches, a few leg cramps. A massage, until this moment, had been a mostly pleasurable experience, a sort of cool-down after Sunday afternoon's game.

But that was before he'd been tossed around the inside of his Ferrari, his shoulder making sharp, repeated contact with the pushed-in passenger-side door, or spent nearly two weeks sitting alone in his condo, his only exercise coming from punching the buttons on the remote control.

For the long minutes it took Taylor to "warm" his muscles, he alternately thought of either leaping from the table or whimpering, or both, and for the past fifteen minutes he'd fought the urge to moan in ecstasy.

The woman had magic hands, capable of inflicting both deep muscle soreness or soothing, strangely provocative pleasure that had him grateful to be lying facedown on the table rather than faceup. When she at last made that evocative trail down his spine with one hand, then held her fingertips against his skin for a few moments, signaling that she was finished with him, he didn't know whether he should say thank-you kindly and crawl away, or offer her a cigarette.

He decided to crawl away. But as he jackknifed to a sitting position, the room spun around a single time and he clutched the ends of the table for support.

"Always sit up slowly after a session, Holden," Taylor told him, already wiping down the doughnut with scented rubbing alcohol. "You've lost all the blood in your head, sitting up so fast."

"And I know just where it all went," he muttered beneath his breath as she turned away to shut off the CD player. How could she pretend to be so indifferent to him? They'd set off sparks on each other from the first moment, and this past half hour had been a living hell of mingled attraction and unbearable tension. Surely he wasn't the only one who felt this way?

"You said something?" Taylor asked as he stood up, pulling the towel with him, holding it in front of himself protectively, trying his best to look nonchalant while he felt like a horny teenager.

"I said, I wonder where Mrs. Helper went. I don't hear her singing anymore," Holden improvised quickly, not really caring where Thelma Helper was as long as she wasn't in the room with him.

"She said something earlier about taking a nap before her soap comes on. She did tell you not to ask her for anything between three and four, didn't she? Now, I want you to drink plenty of water for the remainder of the day—I want you to drink plenty of water every day, actually, to help cleanse your system after I've massaged some of the gunk from your muscles.''

"Gunk? That would be the technical term? I'm very impressed.''

"It's close enough, okay? Now, if you'll let me finish? Tonight I'll show you a few simple exercises you can do on your own, all right? I know I have rubber bands in my case. I think I'll start you with the yellow one. The red one is too easy.''

"Rubber band?'' Holden eyed her owlishly.

"It's just a long, stretchy piece of rubber you use for stretching exercises. Nothing major. People spend entirely too much money on complicated machines and contraptions. A big can of corn, a rubber band—you'd be surprised how much mileage you can get out of just those two things.''

"The imagination runs rampant, truly,'' Holden responded dryly, looking at the clock on the VCR across the room and already wondering what he would do for the remainder of the day. The remainder of the week. The long weeks stretching out ahead of him before he could return to Philadelphia.

And wondering how long it would be before he couldn't keep his hands off the infuriating Miss Taylor Angel.

"You play gin?'' he asked, feeling desperate.

"Penny a point?" she answered immediately, folding up the other towel and laying it on the table. "There's a deck of cards in the upstairs living room. I'll meet you there in ten minutes. Bring your wallet."

"Agreed," Holden said, and quickly left the room so that he didn't have what would have been the pleasant satisfaction of seeing Taylor sag against the edge of the table, roll her eyes heavenward and let out a long, shaky sigh.

HOLDEN WAS DOWN ten dollars and eighty-seven cents when somebody outside started doing a tap dance on a car horn, the noise persisting until he pushed back his chair, a premonition of imminent doom having settled over him, and walked out onto the balcony to see a vintage cherry red Volkswagen convertible with California license plates parked, cockeyed, at the curb.

Inside the Bug were a fluorescent yellow surfboard, a small mountain of designer luggage and a deeply tanned young man with sun-bleached white blond hair and a toothful grin that would rival the brilliance of all of the Osmonds' dental work put together, then squared.

"Woody," Holden breathed quietly, fatalistically, motioning for his stepbrother to both stop leaning on the horn and get himself inside, where he wouldn't scare the locals.

"Woody who?" Taylor asked from behind him, then walked to the white pipe railing and looked down into the street. "Oh, boy. He looks like a commercial for suntan lotion—or the poster boy for Dumb But Beautiful, Incorporated. A blood relative, I presume?"

"Don't be mean. Isn't it enough you're beating the hell out of me at gin?" Holden snapped back, then laughed, as she had been close to correct. "Woody is my stepbrother, actually. Did I mention that he was driving here from Malibu? I didn't expect him yet. He must have broken every speed limit from here to Nevada. Nobody speeds in California, the roads are too crowded."

"No, you didn't mention it," Taylor responded, something very much like disappointment in her tone. "Is he staying long?"

"All summer," Holden told her. "I'm baby-sitting while his daddy revisits his past. You ever hear of Peter LeGrand?"

Taylor's eyebrows climbed almost comically on her forehead. "The rock star? Well, that's one secret you've kept from the media, or at least from the legitimate papers. I don't read the tabloids." She peered over the railing once more. "Son of a gun. He does look sort of like Pistol Pete. Like he did a couple of decades ago, I mean. Shouldn't we have told Thelma he was coming? I don't think she's made up any of the other beds."

"I think Woody could sleep in a bathtub and probably has," Holden said, wincing as Woodstock LeGrand vaulted out of the car without opening the door, displaying a muscle shirt and a pair of psychedelic shorts with a hole just beneath the back pocket. "Where's Tiff?" he then yelled, leaning over the railing.

"Who's Tiff?"

"She's flying in to Philly, then taking a limo! You know how Tiff likes to rough it," Woody, cupping his hands at the sides of his mouth, responded in a near bellow.

"A limo?" Holden repeated, shaking his head. Tiffany certainly had style. Sort of.

"Who's Tiff?"

"If we're lucky, she'll be skyjacked, huh?" Woody offered amicably, if loudly, as he pulled his surfboard out of the back seat.

"She's coming alone, isn't she? She shows up with a beach bum, and you're all outta here!"

"Who is Tiff!"

Holden turned and looked at Taylor, who was looking decidedly mulish. "Huh?"

"I asked, and will repeat for the benefit of the listening audience—which must be half of Ocean City, which you ought to be thinking about if you want to stay anonymous while you're here—*who* is Tiff?"

"My teenage stepsister. And Woody's half sister. Before my mother's time—wives two and three, I think. Mother and Peter lasted about six weeks, but Woody and Tiffany and I, well, I think we've bonded in some strange way. Don't frown," he told her. "I'll draw you a family tree."

"Better have a lot of branches," she quipped, then frowned. "If Woody down there is the older one, how old is this Tiff person? And is she staying here all summer, too? And before you answer—will that be everybody? Or am I not going to be able to tell all the players without a scorecard?"

Holden grinned. "Thought we'd be all alone, did you? Just you and me and this great big condo. I'm flattered. And as disappointed as you, to tell the truth. It could have been fun."

"Go to hell, Holden Masters," Taylor retorted hotly, then stomped back into the living room, leaving him alone to lean against the railing, an absurdly pleased smile on his face.

Maybe he wouldn't have to kill Sid after all....

WOODSTOCK LEGRAND WAS a neat kid, kid being the operative word. Neat was definitely not one of his virtues. Within two hours of his arrival, the condo showed signs of his habitation from kitchen to foyer.

Taylor pushed the boy's surfboard closer to the wall as she headed for the stairs, snagged a muscle shirt from the railing on the between floor where the two smaller bedrooms were located, picked up a sneaker on the way to the upper living room and tripped over a second sneaker as she entered the kitchen—to see Woody perched, barefoot, on the tiled countertop, telling Thelma she should rename her parakeet Louise.

"Get him out of here, would you?" Thelma pleaded, a cigarette clamped between her teeth, the rising smoke forcing her to keep one eye closed—a look that had already put Taylor in mind of Popeye on acid, not that she'd dare to say any such thing to the housekeeper. "They oughta fence in all of California, or so my Sam always said. Not to keep other people out, but to keep the Californians *in*. Nuts—all of them!"

"And sloppy, too," Taylor commented pleasantly, tossing Woody his muscle shirt. "Thelma? Isn't it time for your soap?"

By way of an answer, Thelma took a swipe at Woody with her wet dishcloth and muttered, "Now see what you've done? And Rosemary is going to tell Vanessa that Rob isn't her real father and that's why the kidney has to come from Garth, who Vanessa thinks is her uncle! Stand back, T and A. I'm going to miss the best part!"

"T and A?" Wood repeated, hopping down from the counter even as he picked up his full glass of Thelma's potent iced tea. "That wouldn't be what I think it is, would it?"

"It doesn't stand for tonsils and adenoids," Taylor grumbled, then watched in amazement as Woody chugalugged the entire glass of iced tea without so much as pausing to grimace. "You like that stuff?"

Woody shrugged. "What's not to like? I don't do sugar anymore. Bad for the system—upsets the hell out of the body's natural balances and all that." He frowned, then shrugged. "I think." Then he picked up a knife and sliced himself a man-size hunk of brownie from the pan sitting on the counter.

"What do you think is in brownies, Woody—rutabagas?" Taylor teased, finding it impossible not to like this handsome young specimen with the look of California beaches, the personality of Ronald McDonald and—seemingly—the brainpower of a fruit fly.

Woody frowned at the half-eaten brownie. "Thelma said it was healthful." He looked at Taylor, his innocent blue eyes round with astonishment. "Are you saying she *lied* to me?"

Taylor held up her hands in mock horror. "Don't get me involved in this, Woody," she warned. "I have to work here, and I wouldn't want to get on Thelma's bad side." Then she turned and left the kitchen, having forgotten why she had come upstairs in the first place. Probably to see if Holden's bedroom door was open and ask what he was doing, and then say she was too busy to do it with him.

Probably.

But she had snapped back to her saner self now and should probably go for another run on the beach or something.

Or take another cold shower.

"Hey—are you really Holden's private masseuse?" Woody asked, following her, dripping brownie crumbs like some overgrown puppy with a blue-blood pedigree and in need of training papers.

"Masseuse?" Taylor stopped abruptly, her foot poised over the first step leading down to the living room, so that Woody cannoned into her, nearly sending the two of them flying down the stairs. She whirled around to look up at the young man. "He told you I was his private *masseuse?* And I'll bet he snickered and winked as he said it, didn't he? Why, I'll kill the son of a—"

"Whoa!" Woody interrupted, putting a hand against Taylor's upper chest, holding her back from the mayhem she fully intended to inflict on Holden Masters's superb body. "He didn't say that—I did. Holden said you're his physical and massage therapist. But I thought all therapists had hands like steak platters and names like Bruno or Helga. You're way too pretty to be a therapist. Great legs, you know. And the rest of you isn't too bad, either. Although I guess you are too old for me."

"Centuries too old for you, Woody." Taylor who had just turned twenty-seven, a mere four years older than Woodstock LeGrand, relaxed, wondering why she had gotten so angry so quickly in the first place. She had heard all the "personal masseuse" jokes years ago and had learned to ignore them.

But there was just something about thinking that Holden Masters had made a joke at her expense that—well, she'd just forget it. "Whole centuries, Woody, but thanks for that remark about my legs—and the rest of me," she added, then turned around again to go down the stairs and find a good book to read before dinner.

"You're welcome," Woody answered affably, then did his puppy imitation again, gaily padding after her. "So, you two an item or what? I pretty much knew give-me-lots-of-money Amanda was on her way out. It's been six months, you know. Nobody lasts longer than six months with Holden. You'd think these bloodsuckers would buy a clue, you know, and figure that out."

Taylor stopped dead on the bottom step, turned, placed both hands on the pipe railings on either side of the staircase and effectively blocked Woody from advancing any farther.

"Let's do this all at once, okay?" she began, smiling over gritted teeth. "One, I don't know who Amanda is, don't care who or what you think Amanda is and, if she's smart, she'll dump him before he dumps her. Two, I am here as an employee, period, and do not have designs on your brother, don't want to have designs on your brother, and if your brother has designs on me he's in for a bitter disappointment. This is not Hollywood, or Malibu, or a scene out of Thelma's soap. This is Ocean City, *New Jersey,* for crying out loud, and not some romantic getaway island for swinging singles. Now, you got that, Woody?''

"Well," said a voice from the kitchen level, sending Taylor's heart to her toes even as she looked past Woody LeGrand and straight into the laughing green eyes of Holden Masters, "I don't know if Woody's got that, but I sure heard the message loud and clear. Did you get that message loud and clear, Tiffany?''

"I sure did, Holden." A high-pitched, little-girl voice came from a lower level of the condo, and Taylor quickly peeked over the railing to see a beautiful young female face grinning up at her. "Didn't Spencer Tracy and Katherine Hepburn do that in a movie? Talk like that, you know—all quick and mean and full of put-downs? Maw-maw was always making me watch those old flicks with her. Gee, this is just like a movie, huh? So, who's the blonde?''

"I...want...to...die," Taylor muttered quietly in measured pauses, speaking only to herself, but unfortunately, loudly enough for Holden to hear.

"Why don't you help Tiffany get settled first, Taylor? Talk to her, ask her about her life, her problems with Maw-maw and Daddykins," Holden suggested, laughter in his voice. "If you survive that—

and not many have—then well, there's always that proverbial long walk on a short pier."

"Don't do it, Taylor," Woody warned, moving her hand from the rail so he could get past her. "You may not have had all your shots. Why don't you go for a run on the beach with Holden instead. That's what he said he was going to do. I'll go help Tiff. After all, I've got those eight-by-ten pictures of her in her Snow White costume when she was six. Blackmail may not be pretty, but it's kept me safe for a lot of years."

"You're so full of it, Woodstock!" Tiffany groused, then smiled, showing that the whiter-than-white teeth must be a LeGrand inheritance. "But you could help the chauffeur with the luggage. Oh, and could you tip him, too? I don't have anything smaller than a hundred, I'm afraid."

"Nothing smaller than a hundred?" Taylor repeated, dumbstruck. "How old is that kid?" she asked Holden as he came down the steps.

"Eighteen, going on thirty," he answered, taking her hand. "Come on, let's get out of here while the getting's good. They may be happy now, but they'll be screaming at each other in an hour. Unless they decide to gang up against me, at which point it will be every man and woman for themselves. I'm no hero."

"Really?" Taylor shrugged. "Much as I hate to say it, I'm beginning to think you're a lot nicer than you want me to believe. Either that or you're soft in the head. Do you realize what you're doing, letting those two stay here all summer?''

His grin weakened her knees. "Shooting the hell out of any possible personal love life?" he offered, then ducked as Taylor took a halfhearted swing at him.

As they went down the remainder of the stairs, then sneaked out through the garage entrance to avoid further contact with either Woody or Tiffany, Taylor began to wonder just what in the devil had happened in the past eight hours, ever since the moment she had first laid eyes on Holden Masters. Because, whatever it was, she had a feeling her life would never be the same.

4

MASTERS MISSING, RUMORS RATTLE OWNERS
byline Rich "The Nose" Newsome

Holden Masters, injured in a single car accident nearly a month ago, is still listed among the missing on the roster of Philadelphia's favorite NFL team as preseason training camp sets to open next month.

Masters, we all know, became a free agent at the end of last season, but will a reputed bidding war continue when our local hero is nowhere to be found, his physical condition, or lack of it, still a mystery to team owner Phil Gibbons and the rest of the NFL?

And where is Sidney Feldon, Masters's suddenly shy agent? Is this all a ploy to up the ante? Or has Masters's career been put in jeopardy by an injury he's doing his best to hide? So what's the story, Masters? You "Holden" out on us?

"DID YOU HEAR all of that, Sid?" Holden asked, pacing the living room as he shouted into the speakerphone at Sidney Feldon, who was several thousand miles away in Maui. "Fun's fun and all that, but Newsome is getting mean. I don't like doing this to my team, or to my fans. I want to call it off, now."

Sid's voice boomed into the room, along with the sound of some Hawaiian chant playing along in the background. "Holden, Holden, Holden, you're overreacting. Trust me on this. Everything's fine. I talked to Phil yesterday and assured him you're only taking a well-deserved vacation. Oh, and did I mention that the latest offer has a hell of a bonus that kicks in if you take the team to another Super Bowl in the next three years? So—it's been a while since Taylor started working on you. How is the shoulder anyway?"

Holden smiled across the room at Taylor, who had been working at the table, doing a two-thousand-piece jigsaw puzzle. "Why don't you ask my slave driver, Sid?"

"Taylor? You there, honey?" Sid asked, and Taylor grimaced toward the phone.

"I don't like talking into those speakerphones. It's like talking into an echo chamber," she complained to Holden quietly, then shrugged as Sid called out her name again. "Hi, Sid—I'm here. What do you want to know?"

"It's been over three weeks since the accident, Taylor, honey. How much can I hope to know? If he's behaving, I suppose. That's the most important. Did you have to threaten him with your black belt in karate? And how the shoulder is, of course."

Taylor smiled at Holden, who immediately began advancing on her, making puckering motions with his mouth, then pretending to defend himself from imminent attack. If nothing else, they had, over the past ten days, come to understand each other a little, relax a little in each other's presence, had even begun to joke with one another. It was a nice relationship—when she wasn't dreaming about him, when she wasn't touching him, having his body under her hands, having to concentrate on keeping her professional detachment in light of her growing personal attachment.

"Of course he's behaving himself. And it hasn't been that long since I started working with him, Sid, so don't expect miracles. He's being religious about his exercises, of course," she responded, now glaring at Holden in mock anger as he began pantomiming holding an invisible woman in his arms and kissing her madly.

"Now cut that out!" she growled quietly, hoping Sid couldn't hear, then went on more loudly. "His bruises are about gone. I've worked a lot of the kinks out of his shoulder, and we're into strengthening the muscles now. Oh—and I think I want to renegotiate our little contract. Or haven't you heard about Woody and Tiffany? I want to put in for combat pay."

"Don't listen to her, Sid," Holden said, walking toward the phone. "The kids are on their best behavior. Good talking to you, buddy. Aloha and all that. Call me next week, all right?" Then he pushed the button breaking the connection and turned to Taylor, frowning. "Okay, out with it. What did they do this time?"

Taylor placed another piece into the puzzle. "Nothing much. Tiffany just used my bathroom for this week's application of temporary hair color, because Thelma promised to short-sheet her bed if she got hair dye all over her own bathroom again. It was a twisted sort of logic, but one Thelma probably wouldn't appreciate, so I cleaned up the mess myself. Have you seen Tiffany yet today? She used a pink rinse this time. She looks like she did a three-and-a-half gainer into a cotton-candy machine."

"And Woody?" Holden asked, his grimace showing he was not sure he wanted to hear the answer.

"He wants me to star in a movie he's thinking of making with a bunch of old college pals," Taylor related calmly, delighted to see the pained expression that immediately appeared on Holden's handsome face. "He says it's a sort of art film, but I think the plot is more in line with *Taylor Does Tulsa,* frankly. I thanked him, but then graciously declined. You know, those kids have more money than common sense."

Holden drew his hands into fists at his side. "That idiot needs a keeper!" he exclaimed, looking ready to find Woody and lock him in his room until he grew a brain.

"Relax," Taylor assured him quickly, for she really did like Woody and knew the boy meant no harm. "It's only a passing phase, I'm sure of it. Just this morning, he told me he's thinking seriously about becoming a seal. He is like a fish in the water, I have to give him that."

"A *navy* SEAL? He's got to be kidding!" Holden's tone was incredulous, to say the least.

Taylor nodded, giggling. "I think he was dead serious, actually, although all he said was that he wanted to be a seal. I found myself biting my tongue so that I wouldn't ask him if he thought it might be difficult to learn how to balance the ball on his nose."

Holden let out a roar of amusement, grabbing onto the back of a nearby chair as if to keep himself from falling on the floor convulsed in mirth, and Taylor joined in his easy, infectious laughter.

There had been a lot of laughter over the past two weeks, mingled with a disturbing amount of sexual tension, but Taylor wouldn't have missed a moment of either of them. She and Holden, after those first horribly tense and awkward few days, had fallen into a sort of rhythm, an unspoken understanding that said, yes, they were attracted to each other and, no, neither of them wanted to act on that attraction.

Woody's and Tiffany's presence had made it easier to follow through on this supposed understanding, although Taylor still privately considered those once-a-day massage sessions to be near occasions of sin.

'Hey—what's so funny? What'd I miss?'' Tiffany chirped from the doorway, looking very California and about as erotic as Bambi with a bikini wax as she stood in bare feet, a six-foot, very tan, vacantly grinning boy standing close behind her, his elbows on her bare shoulders as if she were some sort of supporting prop that kept him from falling down.

A quick count told Taylor that the boy had three gold earrings in his left ear—two in his right ear—and she really did long to ask him why he had shaved his hair off all but the very top of his head. "Oh, and this is Lance," Tiffany continued, still chirping in her little-girl voice. "Say hello, Lance."

"Hullo," Lance said obediently, then began rubbing the sides of Tiffany's minuscule waist with his big hands, which brought a low growl out of Holden.

"Lance doesn't know who you are, Holden," Tiffany trilled, putting up a hand to stroke the boy's cheek as he began nibbling at her neck. "Isn't that, like, totally unbelievable?"

Thelma poked her head into the room, talking around her ever-present cigarette. "Get out of that wet bathing suit, young lady, or you'll get a belly-ache. Didn't your mother teach you anything? Oh, and you—Mr. Masters—there's a wash basket in the laundry room. Mostly full of your underwear. Go carry it upstairs, why don't you. It'll be good therapy.''

The housekeeper disappeared before Tiffany could do more than grimace or Holden could say something he'd regret, leaving Taylor to quickly ask Lance if he wanted a glass of iced tea—or did he think he was going to have Tiffany for lunch?

"No, thank you, ma'am," Lance responded, sounding dumb as a clam, but showing enough common sense to disentangle himself from Tiffany's willowy body—and obviously not realizing that calling Taylor "ma'am" had not exactly endeared him to her. "We just ate up on the boardwalk, didn't we, Sugar?"

"Sure did, Love Buns," Tiffany responded, then looked at Holden once more, just as obliviously not noticing that a small tic had begun to work in her stepbrother's left cheek. "Lance knows who Daddykins is, of course, but he doesn't watch sports. Isn't that a kick?"

Lance spread his hands almost apologetically. "I'm, like, just not into that whole team sports scene, you know? I'm saving up to hit all the great surfing spots. You know, like in that *Endless Summer* flick? Caught it on cable, and it's totally rad. You haven't lived 'til you've wiped out in one of those big ones. Waves, that is..." he trailed off, probably realizing that he'd lost his audience—if he'd ever had it. "Well, you know."

"Tiffany, I want to talk to you. Upstairs in my room. *Now*," Holden commanded, walking out of the room without looking at Lance again.

Tiffany shrugged, looking at Taylor. "He's ticked, isn't he?"

"Considering the fact that no one is supposed to know he's here, and you've told Lance and God knows who else—well, yes, Tiffany, I'd say Holden might be just a little bit *ticked*," she answered honestly, then closed her eyes a moment before doing something dumb—volunteering. "Why don't you and Lance go back to the beach, and I'll try to calm him down."

Tiffany sagged, bent kneed, faking a faint—a typically melodramatic Tiffany response—then recovered just as quickly. "You'd do that for me? Holden can be *such* a bear, you know. How can I thank you?"

"You can send my body back home to Mom and Dad in Pennsylvania," Taylor mumbled to the thin air, because Tiffany and Lance—who couldn't be as dumb as he looked, or talked—were already halfway down the stairs, rapidly making their escape.

HOLDEN HEARD THE KNOCK and turned around as the door opened, running his left hand through his hair. "Tiffany, we both know you've pulled some dumb

stunts in the past, but—'' He broke off when he saw
Taylor standing there. "It figures," he said flatly.
"What did she do, hop on Love Buns's back and tell
him to giddyap, getting her away from her pain-in-
the-neck big brother?"

"I told her to go," Taylor said, walking over to the
bed and sitting down on the edge of the mattress.
"My first aid is pretty rusty, and I had a feeling you
weren't going to be kind."

Holden stared at her, goggle-eyed. "Kind? *Kind?*
Do you know what she did?" he asked, pointing in
the general direction of the front of the house and the
beach, where Tiffany was probably already quite
happily forgetting the consequences she had so re-
cently escaped. "Why doesn't she just rent one of
those sign-bearing planes that fly past here all day and
send it up and down the coast, advertising our address? Sid is going to have a cow."

"A whole cow? Well now, I'd pay down real cash
money to watch that," Taylor remarked, pulling an
emery board out of her shorts pocket and beginning
to file her already short, neatly rounded nails, ap-
pearing as calm and unflustered as he felt hot and
bothered. "Give yourself a moment to think about
this, Holden, why don't you? You just got off the
phone with Sid after telling him you didn't want any
more stories from that 'nose' guy. You told Sid you
didn't like all this secrecy. And I don't blame you.
You're not one hundred percent yet—that's a few

weeks away—but you're good enough to face a few reporters and cameras. So, what's the big deal?''

He spoke slowly as if speaking to a child. ''The big deal, Taylor, is that the best defense is still a good offense. *We* want to make any announcements to the press, picking our own time, our own place. Which we're probably going to have to do now, before our resident Atlantic-to-Pacific big mouth plays whisper down the beach to anyone who'll listen, until we find a dozen reporters and cameras parked outside our front door.''

''Oh,'' Taylor said, replacing the emery board in her pocket. ''Well, that makes sense. You going to call Sid? If you do, please put him on the speaker again. I love to hear people sputter.''

''I *told* him this was a bad idea,'' Holden said, talking mostly to himself. ''I didn't like it from the beginning. Must have been those painkillers they gave me at the hospital. Yes, that's it. I wasn't in my right mind when I agreed to this idiocy. And how do I explain Taylor away, when Sid says I'm just vacationing with my family, or whatever lie he's going to tell?''

''Maybe *Taylor* can just fold her massage table and steal away into the night? Maybe you can do the rest of your therapy on your own? I sure won't cry over that decision,'' Taylor suggested quietly, although he could detect an edge of anger in her voice.

"What?" Holden whirled around, looking at Taylor as she sat on the bed, sat on *his* bed, where he lay awake at night, every night, wanting her beside him. "No," he said quickly, "I need you here."

Taylor shrugged. "If you insist. I suppose you could tell the reporters I'm a friend of Tiffany's? Or maybe even Woody's girlfriend?"

Holden grimaced. "Nobody would believe either story. Besides, I couldn't tell either lie with a straight face. Unless, maybe, you were to dye your hair green and only speak in words of one syllable?"

"Funny," Taylor said, rising to her feet and walking to the sliding glass door that looked out over his private balcony and a less than sterling view of the alley and all the recycling garbage cans. "Well, do what you want, as long as you've decided to end the secrecy bit. It was all just a little too cloak-and-dagger to suit me anyway. Could I use your whirlpool tonight? I've got a couple of kinks hanging around after our run this morning."

God had to be punishing him for some forgotten misdeed. It was the only explanation. The thought of Taylor in his bathroom, in his whirlpool, made his throat go dry—and brought out a little bit of the devil that had been in him these past two weeks. "It's big enough for two, you know," he said, walking up behind her and putting his hands on her upper arms.

"Holden..." she said warningly, then let her voice trail off as he bent forward and pressed his lips against the side of her throat, using more finesse than Love Buns, but feeling all the swift sexual passion of any hormonally charged teenage boy.

"Hm...?" he answered, sliding his hands down her arms to her elbows and then splaying them against her flat stomach. He would have said more, said something low and hopefully sexy, but he was having considerable difficulty in swallowing. And thinking.

"We can't do this," Taylor told him, although he was still clearheaded enough to know that she might be protesting, but she wasn't moving. In fact, she was melting against him. "You're my employer."

"Sid hired you, not me."

"You know what I mean," she persisted even as he blazed a trail from the tender skin beneath her ear all the way to the collar of her soft cotton shirt. Her breath became audible as she blew it out in a long, ragged sigh that did wonders for his ego.

When she spoke again, it was rapidly, as if she was trying to say the words as quickly as she could, while they both still believed them. "I'm your therapist. You're my client. We have a strictly professional relationship that can't be forgotten just because we have this...this mutual physical attraction. There's... there's ethics...and there's...there's...oh, the *hell* with it!"

She turned in his arms and grabbed his face between her hands, yanking his head down so that his mouth crashed against hers.

He needed no further encouragement, pulling her hard against the length of his body as her fingers tangled in his hair, urging her lips open so that he could deepen their kiss. He felt like an animal, like they were both animals, set to devour each other to satisfy appetites too long denied.

His hands stroked the length of her back, cupped her buttocks as he pulled her even closer, then eased her slightly away from him, their mouths still locked together as he bent forward slightly so his hands could skim the flatness of her stomach, cup the fullness of her breasts—all as her hands were working on the front button of his shorts and as he began maneuvering her toward the bed.

"Holden! Who *is* that woman?"

Holden froze in the act of unbuttoning the top button of Taylor's shirt, his eyes popping open at the sound of a very distinctive, husky female voice. "Somebody has put a curse on me," he mumbled in disbelief, his lips still mostly clinging to Taylor's.

He put his hands on Taylor's shoulders and disengaged himself reluctantly—oh, so reluctantly—then carefully placed her behind him protectively as he turned to smile at the latest in a long line of beautiful, supposedly disposable women who stood just inside the door that should have been closed.

"Why, hello, Amanda. What brings you to Ocean City?" he asked brightly, knowing he was a dead man.

IT HAD BEEN OVER two hours since Amanda Price had made her entrance. Taylor had spent the time sitting on a towel she'd laid on the nearly deserted beach, silently calling herself every kind of fool she could imagine and then some she couldn't.

How could she have been so stupid? So *irresponsible?* So horribly unprofessional?

Why had she gone to the man's room in the first place, knowing how attracted she was to him?

How could she have allowed him to tear down all the barriers she had been carefully building against him these past two weeks?

How could she have been so careless as to *not* close the door behind her!

No. No, she'd skip that last part. She couldn't think like that. It was *good* that she had left the door open. Good. Fortunate. Lucky, even. Why, she should consider Amanda's interruption to have saved her from making the second biggest mistake in her life— Geoff, the playboy golf pro, having been the first four years ago. She certainly didn't need to have her second love affair be with Holden, the playboy quarterback. Some lessons shouldn't have to be learned twice!

However, if Amanda Price hadn't come along, then surely Thelma would have, or Woody. That would have been a lot worse than having supermodel Amanda Price and her expensive clothes, beautiful yet strangely expressionless face and choking perfume stumble over her and Holden as they were about to do something she'd simply rather not think about right now.

"She's gone finally, back to her hotel," Holden said from above and behind her, then sat down beside her on the sand, his long, bare legs stretched out in front of him. He had the straightest legs she'd ever seen, tanned now, and covered with rapidly blonding hair, even though the hair on his head was dark as night.

How she longed to touch him!

Taylor closed her eyes. "What did you say to her?" she asked, not really wanting to know. After all, the woman had ignored her as if she didn't exist, walking into Holden's bedroom and draping herself over his arm, telling him he had been a naughty boy to have gone off without telling her where she could find him when she got back from her swimwear shoot in the Virgin Islands.

Lucky for her, the model had gone on saying, there had been a small item in the New York papers this morning, saying that Woody and Tiffany LeGrand, children of Peter LeGrand, had been seen cavorting on the beaches in Ocean City, New Jersey, of all places.

"You'd said something to me about Woody spending the summer with you when you turned down my invitation to Rome. So I took a chance and called out to California, and the housekeeper gave me this address," she'd explained as she dragged Holden through the kitchen and down the steps to the upper living room, away from Taylor. "Aren't you proud of me, Holden? I'm a budding detective! Now, tell me all about your arm. Is it true that you need major surgery on something called your rotator cuff—and that your career may be over?"

"I guess I hadn't realized the rumors had gotten so bad, so blown out of proportion," Taylor said now, pushing her bare toes into the cooling sand, wondering just how long it would take to dig herself a hole deep enough to bury herself in. Or was she the only one who remembered what had almost happened in Holden's bedroom? Besides, if he dared to try apologizing for having kissed her, she'd have to slug him. It was better to talk about Amanda and the press, and leave the subject of that fairly explosive interlude to die a natural death. "Did you convince Amanda that you don't need surgery?"

"I did."

She laid her elbows on her bent knees and stared out at the ocean as sea gulls laughed overhead, mocking her nervousness. "And did you tell her you're just fine, that your career isn't in jeopardy?"

"That, too."

Why was he talking to her in shorthand—barely getting out more than two words at a time? Something else was wrong. She was sure of it.

Taylor turned her head, rested her chin against her upper arm and looked at Holden out of the corner of her eye. Oh, yeah. Something else was wrong, all right. That tic was working in his left cheek again.

"What else did you tell her?" she asked, feeling an apprehensive knot beginning to tighten in her stomach. "I mean, how did you explain me? Explain, um, what we were doing?"

"Oh, that was simple enough," he said, still speaking in a monotone and still not looking at her. "I told her we'd just gotten engaged."

5

"EXCUSE ME? I COULDN'T have heard that right. You told her *what?*"

Holden grinned, having already figured that it wouldn't take long for Taylor to respond to his last statement. And she hadn't immediately smacked him one across the face and stomped back to the condo to pack her bags. He had to consider that a plus. "I told her she caught us celebrating our engagement. Don't look at me like that—it was the only thing I could think of on such short notice. After all, she did find us in a rather, um, *compromising* position, so I had to protect you."

"Rather compromising? Holden, don't pretty it up on my account. I know what we were doing. We were about to go at each other like crazed rabbits. And you had to protect me? Well, isn't that so wonderfully old-world of you. Who said chivalry was dead? They certainly haven't met Holden Masters, have they?"

She was onto him. Well, he'd always known she wasn't stupid. "All right, all right," he confessed quickly, "so I was also thinking of what Amanda might babble to the press about why you're here. I admit it. Amanda is a lot of things—one of them isn't smart, if you were wondering—but she knows a million people and has a remarkably big mouth. But I *was* worried about your reputation. That was the first thing I thought of, honest." He tried for a smile as he pretended to ward off a physical attack. "You can thank me any way you wish."

"Really? Okay. How about with a hot poker down your shorts?" Taylor suggested, leaping to her feet in one fluid, graceful motion and setting off down the beach.

Holden watched in admiration for a few moments, then went after her because he really did like her. He really did care what she thought about him. And he really, really wanted to explore that "crazed rabbit" attraction Amanda had so rudely interrupted.

"Look, Taylor, it's no big deal. I already called Sid in Maui, and he's going to fax some trumped-up story out to the media. Holden Masters, siblings in tow, is vacationing at an undisclosed New Jersey resort with his loving fiancée. I'm protected from any more rumors on my physical condition. You're protected from Amanda's flapping tongue. It'll all blow over in a couple of days. All right, maybe in a couple of weeks. By the time I sign my new contract tops."

"And, as an added bonus, you get rid of Amanda the Beautiful just as her customary six months are up. You forgot to mention that," Taylor added sarcastically, making him wince as her verbal arrow struck home. "So I guess—as we're doing time lines here— this also means our bogus engagement will be history by, oh, Christmas? At least I have *something* to look forward to, I suppose. I wonder if my parents will be equally as thrilled?"

"Your parents?" Holden winced again. "I hadn't thought about your parents, Taylor. I'm sorry."

"Don't be," she responded, still walking and with enough built-up energy radiating from her tall, slim body that she probably could make it all the way up the coast to Atlantic City without breathing hard. "I'll call them later and explain everything, listen to yet another lecture on why I should never have left Allentown for a return to the big city of Manhattan and then promise to call them next week. What about your mother?"

"Miranda?" Holden hadn't given his mother's re- action a second thought—even a first one. "I don't know. She'll probably beg me not to make her a grandmother yet, then send us something from Bloomingdale's. You like ostentatious crystal bowls?"

"Don't pretend to be dense, Holden. It doesn't become you."

He reached out and took her hand, pulling her to a stop at the water's edge, as she had made a sharp right turn as if intending to walk into the ocean and swim to England. "Look, Taylor," he said seriously, swinging her around to face him, "I don't like this any better than you do. But it was all I could think of, honestly. I only think fast on my feet when a three-hundred-and-fifty-pound defensive end is bearing down on me."

"Oh, sure, expect me to believe that. I'm not Amanda Price, remember," Taylor countered, pulling her hand free of his. "You graduated top of your class in media communications, bucko, so don't act like you can't add two and two."

Holden grinned. "Did your research on me, huh? I'm flattered."

"Don't be," she said, picking up a clamshell and sending it out over the breaking waves before turning away from the water. "So—how long do we have until 'The Nose' finds us?"

"Then you're going to go along with it?" Holden asked in impossible-to-hide relief, following her again and feeling like a puppy who'd messed the new carpet and was now trying to make up for his mistake by being extremely lovable. "Sid did say it was the perfect press release to get me back in the news in a favorable light, get me out of this stupid role of secrecy he put me into and still keep the negotiations on the front burner. So it's working out all around. I get my therapy, you get a small vacation—because I am getting much better, don't you think?—and everything ends happily. I can't thank you enough, Taylor. Honestly."

"First Tiffany, and now you and Uncle Sid," Taylor said, finally smiling, so that he could begin to relax. "By the time this summer is over, you're all going to owe me a small fortune in favors."

THEY OWED HER a small fortune in favors before supper that night as it turned out, simply because she didn't kill Holden Masters, star quarterback, loving brother and chivalrous idiot extraordinaire.

Because, when Taylor and Holden finally left the beach and turned the corner at the end of the row of beachfront condos, it was to see two huge news vans parked outside the lime stucco building and the pavement littered with miles of electrical wire, cameras and a half-dozen television newsmen and print reporters.

Above them, a red-faced Thelma Helper danced around on the upper living-room deck, waving a broom in the air as she yelled at them all to go away before she poured boiling water on them, the way she would drown ants.

"That agent of mine is too much. He must have gotten on the wire the minute the two of us hung up," Holden complained, squeezing Taylor's hand as she slipped it into his, probably not realizing what she was doing—not that he minded. "Just smile pretty and let me do the talking, all right?"

"I already tried that once today, Holden, and ended up engaged to you," she reminded him sharply.

"Much more talking on your end and I'll find myself the clandestine mother of triplets. Please, forgive me if I'm lacking some confidence in my bigmouthed fiancé right now."

"Good point. Triplets, huh? That's too much, even for me. Okay, what else do you suggest? We camp out on the beach all night, hoping they give up and go away? They won't, you know, and the sand flies can get pretty hungry after dark."

Anything Taylor might have suggested meant nothing as one of the reporters shouted out, "There they are!" and Holden gave her hand another squeeze before leading her across the street and straight into contact with the wing-flapping media vultures.

"This the lucky lady, Holden?"

"Where did you meet?"

"What happened to the mustache? You *were* hiding, weren't you?"

"Tell me about the accident, Holden. Is it true you were drunk?"

"Turn this way, Ms. Angel."

"Over here, Taylor, baby. Give us a big smile for the camera!"

"Should I call the police, Mr. Masters? Maybe they'll hit 'em all with billy clubs or something. I'd give up my soap to watch that!"

Holden held up a hand, asking everyone to be silent for a moment as he had an announcement. "Those cameras on?" he asked, wishing Thelma, who was now shouting 911 at the top of her lungs, would just shut up and go back inside the condo.

"Now," he said, smiling as the reporters stepped back a pace, acting only slightly less like piranhas than they had a moment earlier. A boom mike almost got away from one of the technicians, nearly taking off the top of Holden's head. Finally, order was restored—sort of.

"You've got me, guys, so I might as well talk, huh? Here it is, the whole truth. I'm fine. My shoulder is fine—I was dented a little in the accident, but the Ferrari got the worst of it. I'm just a man in love, that's all. Taylor and I tried to get away from the limelight for a little while—get to know each other better—but as long as you're here, I'm happy to announce that, yes, Taylor and I are engaged to be married. We—"

"Nancy Marsh here, local stringer for AP. These guys can talk all the football they want later. Let's just cut to the chase now, okay? That her real name, Holden? *Angel?* Yeah, like anyone's gonna believe that one! Who is she, really? Where did you two meet? What does she do? And what about Amanda Price? She's registered at the Regency right down the street, you know. Isn't that just a little too *cozy?*"

Holden looked at the ambitious woman who had rattled off this list of questions, smiling even as he wondered who in hell she was. "Amanda Price has always been a good friend," he said evenly.

"Uh-huh, sure, feed me that same tired line. I'll bite," the reporter answered archly, scribbling on a steno pad. "Now, Ms. Angel—how do you feel about Holden's good friend Amanda?"

"Well, for one, Nancy, I think she's much more well-mannered than you," Taylor responded, smiling directly into one of the television cameras.

"Easy, Taylor," Holden whispered. "Not nice to poke sticks in reporters' cages. Even the baby ones have big teeth."

"Maybe it's not," Taylor answered, also in a whisper, and also while still smiling, "but it's fun. What's she going to do, tell her readers I said she was rude?"

"You'll wish that was all she writes," he said against Taylor's ear, hearing the click of the cameras as the photographers snapped pictures of the two lovebirds as if they were whispering sweet nothings to each other. "All right, guys," he said then, as the questions started all over again, "if you want anything else, you'll have to go through Sid. He knows everything. For now, how about you give us a little break and a little privacy?"

Just as Holden was guiding Taylor past the line of cameras, thinking they had come away from their first confrontation with the press relatively unscathed, a car pulled to a screeching halt at the curb and Rich "The Nose" Newsome hopped out, as welcome as a plague in May—or any other time.

"So what did you do, Rich?" Holden asked, looking at his longtime nemesis, the sports columnist who had taken an instant dislike to Holden—why, he'd never know—the minute he'd signed with the Philadelphia team eleven years ago. "Rent a helicopter?"

"Ha-ha, Masters. You're a funny man," Newsome responded nastily, bounding over the curb and across the grass to stick a miniature tape recorder right up under Holden's nose. "Before you go scurrying back to your love nest, how about you explain why Ms. Taylor Angel is listed in the New York City telephone directory as a professional masseuse?"

"Who *is* this guy?" Taylor snapped, and Holden felt the first small ground-shakings of rapidly impending doom. "Look, buddy," she said before he could stop her, pointing a finger at Rich Newsome, "that's licensed physical therapist and licensed massage therapist, and that's what it says both in the Manhattan phone book and on my licenses. Get your facts straight, okay?"

"Massage therapist, huh?" Newsome countered, his grin so oily Holden was surprised it didn't slide right off his face. "From Manhattan, too, just where I found your name when I did a little quick research. So, tell me again, off the record, of course—what block of Forty-second Street do you work on, honey? I might want you to run those pretty hands over me someday. How much? Fifty bucks cover an hour alone with the lovely Ms. Angel?"

TAYLOR KEPT MASSAGING Holden's right hand, gently pulling on his fingers one at a time, working the soreness out of his knuckles. "You shouldn't have hit him, you know. That was really dumb, dumber than my dig at that Nancy woman. And it was all my fault. I shouldn't have gotten angry in the first place. After all, I'm used to snide remarks from jerks when my profession is mentioned."

Holden pulled his hand away from hers and fell back against the couch, looking so sweet and vulnerable that she longed to kiss him. Which was a dangerously stupid reaction. "He as good as called you some sort of hooker, Taylor. And not even a high-priced one. What did you expect me to do—give him a cookie?"

She reached up to begin working out the knots in his right shoulder, although he hadn't complained about any soreness. She just knew his body now, knew it probably better than he did himself, and although he had delivered a remarkably fine right across to Rich "The Nose" Newsome's kisser, his arm still wasn't in any shape for such heroic displays. "It's too late for a cookie. Although you might want to send him a three-pound, raw porterhouse steak. His eye was already beginning to swell up before he hit the pavement."

Holden closed his eyes and chuckled. "He's been asking for that for years. And every wonderful bit of it got caught on camera. I guess that will put the kibosh to all that talk about my arm. Sid will be on the phone from Maui pretty soon, screaming that I just threw a million-dollar punch and raking me over the coals for blowing the lid off his little scheme to keep the owners in the dark about what I'm doing."

"Boy, Masters," Taylor said, shaking her head, "when you're wrong, you're *wrong*. Uncle Sid called while you were in the shower. He says your price just went *up*, and that three other teams have already called, wanting to join the bidding. And there's more, Holden. Fast on his feet, Uncle Sid is. He also wants you to put your arm in a sling, then blame Newsome for your *new* injury."

Holden jackknifed to the edge of the couch. "He said *what?* I don't believe that guy! I'm just lucky if The Nose doesn't decide to press charges."

"Don't worry. I talked uncle Sid out of it. And Newsome isn't going to press charges. He's going to crucify you in his column, just like he always does— or so Uncle Sid says. Now," Taylor said, rising from the couch and walking over to lean her hip against the massage table, "how do we call off this so-called engagement? I mean, we don't need this charade anymore, do we?"

He looked at her for long moments, moments during which she was grateful the massage table was there to support her suddenly shaky legs. "Can't do it, Taylor. Not yet. Newsome let everyone know your occupation, remember? If we tell the truth now, the whole world will be jumping down our throats, knowing I was trying to hide this injury. Damn Sid and his big ideas!'' He dropped his head into his hands, stabbing his fingers through his dark hair. ''Why do I feel like we're in a bad sitcom?''

''Because we are, I suppose,'' Taylor told him sympathetically, forgetting for a moment just how angry she should be with him. ''However, if you think we have to keep up this charade until the beginning of August, you'd better have a small talk with Thelma. She's not buying a word of the story Sid put out to the press. She said, and I quote, 'I know how many beds I'm making up each morning.' ''

''Beds? What do beds have to do with—oh.'' Holden grinned. ''And I thought our dear, sweet Mrs. Helper was a proper chain-smoking old lady who wouldn't have such thoughts.''

''She watches daytime soaps, Holden,'' Taylor replied, feeling her own mood beginning to lighten. ''There's *nothing* Thelma doesn't think about. Oh, and she wants a raise, retroactive to her first day on the job. She said Sam would expect her to ask for one, and she wants the money for some new clothing and to get her hair done, just in case the cameras come back. So how does it feel to be blackmailed by one of the senior set?''

And that, Taylor would remember later, was probably the moment she fell unwittingly, carelessly, unreservedly in love with Holden Masters. Because he

listened to what she had to say about Thelma and
then collapsed against the back of the couch, his long,
straight legs splayed out in front of him, and laughed
until tears rolled down his face.

HOLDEN WAS SITTING on the rooftop deck looking up
at the stars, listening to the waves crashing on the
beach a half block away—and wondering how a nice
guy like him ever got caught up in a mess like this—
when Woody found him around ten o'clock that
night.

His stepbrother looked like a character out of some
cartoon, only his whiter-than-white teeth, blond-
streaked hair, the whites of his eyes and the glowing
green face of his wristwatch visible in the pale light
coming from the street lamp as he sat down on the
cool roof, his legs crossed, his elbows on his knees.
"Had yourself a real beaut of a day, didn't you? Tiff
and I just got home—she wouldn't leave the arcade
until she beat my score on this great simulated race-
course—but we met Thelma on her way home to feed
Killer. Man, is she ever on a roll—talking a mile a
minute, even giving instant replays of the big hit. Sam
boxed in the navy, you know. We really missed the
fun, didn't we?"

"Be happy, Woody," Holden told him, lifting a lit
cigar to his mouth and clamping it between his teeth.
He only smoked cigars, only occasionally and only in
the off-season, but this seemed like a good time for

indulging in some sort of vice. At least it kept him from going down to Taylor's room and making a total ass out of himself—as if he could possibly top this afternoon's performance. "You may even want to have a T-shirt made up, saying, 'I survived the Holden Masters punch-out.' Although you might want to head back downstairs pretty soon and catch the news, as I'm pretty sure this is one of those 'film at eleven' stories."

"That's okay. When you've seen as many clips of old Peter flinging guitars and fists as I have, you get sorta jaded, you know? Tiff's in heaven, by the way. She's downstairs with Taylor, talking wedding gowns. Seems she saw a picture of some dame who wore a flesh-colored skintight leather leotard under a big white net cage and thinks Taylor would look great in it. I don't think Taylor was impressed. You know, I thought there was something going on between you two. I mean, all that time alone on the beach and with you on the massage table?"

"We run on the beach every day to keep my legs in shape, and I'm on that massage table to get my muscles loose."

"Uh-huh. Sure. So when's the wedding? You think Peter and the guys will play at the reception? Man, you're going to have to rent Madison Square Garden for all the people and press."

"There isn't going to be—" Holden began, then quickly shut his mouth. Woody was a good kid, but a secret was no safer with him than it would be with Tiffany or Rich Newsome. "That is, Taylor and I don't want a big show, Woody. We want to keep it private, you know. Maybe even fly to Vegas some weekend and do it there. So don't go planning anything, all right? And for God's sake, tell Tiffany to take a breath and step back. Hasn't she been through enough weddings with Daddykins and Maw-maw to have lost the enthusiasm for another one?"

Woody shrugged his shoulders, then pulled a stick of beef jerky out of his shorts pocket and began gnawing on it. "There's something fishy here, Holden," he said after a moment, causing his stepbrother to look at him warily. "I mean, aren't you supposed to be all happy and sappy? I mean, like you just got engaged. And where's the ring? Peter gave the child bride a three-carat diamond she could use as a paperweight. It's not like you to be a cheapskate, Holden. Or was this just so quick you didn't have time to do it right?"

A ring. Holden shut his eyes, feeling the six-story drop just in front of his make-it-up-as-you-go-along plan becoming more like he was about to take a swan dive off the Empire State Building. He hadn't thought about a ring. He hadn't thought about much of anything, when you got right down to it, other than how good Taylor had felt in his arms after two weeks of the most incredible physical attraction he'd ever encountered, how right. And how he could ever possibly get her back there again without leading her to believe this mock engagement might actually have a future. Which it didn't, of course.

Because he was not, never was, never would be the marrying kind, not with the evidence of Peter's and Miranda's combined track records to scare him off the idea. Not that marrying Taylor Angel was even within the realm of possibility, even if he did decide to settle down one day—at least a decade from now—succumbing to some as yet unfelt need for a couple of kids of his own.

But he'd bet she'd make great kids if they were anything like their mother.

Now cut that out! he screamed silently, nearly biting the end off his two-dollar cigar.

All right. So Taylor was beautiful. And funny. And intelligent. And gutsy. And not a bit afraid of or impressed by him, his reputation or his money. That didn't mean anything. Wanting her in his bed meant something—but that something wasn't love. It was desire, pure and simple. The gut-wrenching pain he'd unexpectedly felt earlier, when she suggested that they put an end to the sham and she leave Ocean City, leave *him*—well, that had just been some stupid aberration, a fleeting fear that he'd have to deal with explaining her departure to the press.

That's all.

Nothing more.

Taylor Angel was no more than a fairly enjoyable moment in time, a temporary attraction he'd overcome the minute he was back in circulation, a beautiful pain in the neck who used a little Yanni, a little scented oil, a little blood-heating massage to drive him out of his mind, then filling that same mind with thoughts that would make even Thelma Helper blush.

"So? You getting her a ring or what?" Woody persisted when his stepbrother didn't answer him.

"Yeah, Woody. I'll get her a ring," Holden said fatalistically, making up his mind. "My cover's blown anyway, so I guess we can all drive up to Atlantic City tomorrow. We're bound to find a suitable paperweight in one of the casino jewelry stores."

"The casinos! All right!" Woody leaped to his feet. "Of course, Tiffany isn't old enough to get in to gamble, you know. But she'll want to go to the shops. Then we can have dinner at one of the steak houses—they do have steak houses, don't they? Man, you know what, Holden? This is gonna be neat. Really neat. Taylor's so, like, well, *normal*—not like Peter's wives. I don't think Tiff and I really ever had that. We can actually do things together with Taylor—play gin, do jigsaw puzzles, eat dinner together, talk about stuff. Just like a real family, you know?"

Holden took a deep pull on his cigar, blew out a thin stream of blue smoke. "Yeah, Woody, just like a real family.'' He closed his eyes on Woody's youthful, hopeful smile, deciding he had a problem on his hands. Yeah. He had a *real* problem....

6

DAWN OF THE DAY AFTER her "engagement" announcement arrived—baffling Taylor, who felt sure the world would come to a merciful end sometime during the night—and she dragged herself out of bed for her morning run, hoping to leave before Holden could join her.

Her luck, which hadn't been good, definitely hadn't improved overnight.

"You ready?" Holden asked easily, doing some muscle stretches against one of the porch poles as she closed the door to the condo and just before she could breathe a sigh of relief at getting out of the house without running into anyone.

She looked at him in the yellow glow from the porch light, for the sun had yet to break over the water and erase the gray of dawn, his palms pressed against the pillar. He had his left knee bent, his right leg stuck out behind him, giving his Achilles tendon full extension—and giving her a truly remarkable view of his white-running-shorts-clad rear end. The man was a near god. Perfect form. Perfect muscular delineation—not too "stringy," not too muscle-bound. Perfect tan. Perfect teeth. Perfect hair. Perfect face.

Perfectly infuriating.

"Aren't you afraid some reporter is lurking in the hydrangeas?" she asked, voicing her own private fears aloud. She definitely did not like being in the public eye, at least not when she wasn't prepared for the exposure.

"The sun isn't up yet, Taylor," he said, grinning at her. "They're probably still all hanging upside down in their caves, sipping coffee through straws. Although one of our neighbors just jogged by a couple of minutes ago to say he saw us on television last night. Thinks I'm a lucky, lucky man—then had me sign his sneaker."

Taylor sniffed as she began doing a few stretches of her own, never realizing that watching her body in motion could be as interesting to Holden as his exercises had been to her. "You are a lucky man. You're still alive."

"Now, now, be nice, Taylor," Holden said as they walked down the path to the sidewalk, heading for the beach to start their run. "After all, you're going to have to unclench those fists long enough for me to slip a ring on your finger."

Taylor stumbled over a nonexistent bump in the sidewalk and nearly went sprawling before Holden caught her. This was going on too long, going to far— and she was going to put a stop to it, just as soon as she figured out how. "There will be no ring," she told him, suddenly breathless, not to mention nervous. "No ring, no engagement party, and definitely no flesh-colored leather wedding leotard. Or haven't you heard that one yet?"

"Tiffany," he said, rolling his eyes as they climbed over the path cut into the dunes and entered the wide, deserted beach area. "She's got a vivid imagination."

"She also has green hair, or so she promised before she went to bed last night. And another hole in her ear, courtesy of Honey Buns and his handy-dandy ear-piercing punch—he has his own, you understand. I like Tiffany, like her very much, but somebody has to sit on that kid—and soon."

"Love Buns."

Taylor looked at him quizzically as they neared the water's edge, the rising sun painting a golden stripe from the horizon to the shore, turned toward the sky blue water tower in the distance and began to jog on the wet sand. "What?"

"*Love* Buns," Holden repeated. "You called Lance *Honey* Buns. But that's all right. Anybody can make a mistake."

"*Lance* is a mistake," Taylor groused, her ponytail slapping back and forth behind her as she lowered her head, ready to break into her first full-out run that would last a good two hundred yards. "But then, I imagine she's only following in her father's footsteps. It's a shame. Now, I'm out of here!''

HOLDEN LET HER GET a head start, because he could outrun her easily and because he enjoyed watching the way she moved—gracefully, like a young gazelle, all golden tan and honey hair, unaware or uncaring of her own beauty, her own attraction.

Then, feeling the need to burn up some excess energy, he slowly accelerated, running as if the entire Dallas Cowboys defense was after him, holding an imaginary ball to his chest with his left hand, his right arm held out straight. He zigzagged down the beach, not stopping until he crossed the width of the sand to collapse on the steps leading to the very beginning of the boardwalk.

Breathing heavily, and with his right shoulder aching—not that he'd tell Taylor that—he lowered his head to his bent knees and took in huge gulps of air, trying to slow his heartbeat.

''Show-off,'' Taylor said a few moments later, collapsing beside him on the wooden steps.

''Show-off? What do you mean? I was just getting some of the kinks out.''

''Sure,'' Taylor agreed facetiously. ''And those three drooling women up there behind us, freezing their very visible buns off trying to impress you, had nothing to do with those moves you were putting on, huh? I kept waiting for you to stiff-arm a sea gull, then spike the ball in the end zone."

Holden tipped his head back and looked up at the boardwalk. Sure enough, there stood three very lovely, very young, bikini-clad ladies posing against the railing. They immediately called to him by name and waved to him.

Obviously, his presence in Ocean City had hit all the television stations, and the newspapers, as well.

"Son of a gun," he said, waving back, knowing he *always* noticed beautiful women. "I didn't even see them. Must be getting old." And then he frowned. *Why hadn't* he seen them? *Because you were too busy looking at Taylor Angel, that's why,* he told himself.

"So," he ventured swiftly, preferring not to investigate that particular thought any longer, "you think you're up for a trip to Atlantic City? I know I could use a break. All exercise and no play makes Holden a dull boy, you know."

"If I could believe that, I'd have you working out ten hours a day," Taylor groused, bending down to rub at a sudden cramp in her calf.

"Here, let me help you," Holden offered, dropping to his knees in the sand in front of her and taking her calf in both hands. "Push down with your heel while I rub toward your heart. It helps, honest."

He began stroking her calf, his fingers skimming over the silky smoothness, his mind skipping over possibilities he'd be safer not supposing. He could feel the cramp slowly beginning to leave the muscle and smiled up at Taylor.

"See? Told you it works, or did you think you were the only one who had a way with a muscle?" he teased.

His grin broadened as he saw the way Taylor was looking at him—the way her eyes looked all warm and soft for a moment before she pulled her leg free with a curt "Thanks" and started back up the beach toward the condo.

"Who's going to Atlantic City?" she asked, keeping to a slow jog. "Tiffany isn't old enough to gamble, you know, not that she's going to be happy to hear that."

"She'll be happy enough buying out half the stores," Holden told her, also content to keep to a slow jog. His heart rate was plenty high as it was, thank you, and his hands still tingled with awareness after massaging Taylor's shapely calf.

Did she ever feel that way when she was working on him? No, she couldn't. Nobody could feel the way he did and keep it a secret for long. Or not want to progress to the next level of attraction. "Amanda will keep her company," he added, making up his mind to invite his old girlfriend along, probably for his own protection.

Taylor's ponytail slapped against the side of her head as she turned to look at him. "Amanda Price is going with us?" she asked, sounding disappointed for a moment before she shrugged. "Want to keep up the lover-boy image, I suppose. It figures. Just as long as I don't go picking up some tabloid that has 'Masters Engaged, Still Making Moves' in three-inch headlines. Mother and Dad would be *so* upset for their little girl."

"You're still mad, aren't you?" Holden asked, knowing it was a stupid question—even if it was the same stupid question he'd been longing to ask her all morning. "You know I didn't plan this, Taylor. It just—well, it just sort of *happened,* that's all."

"Open mouth, insert foot, huh, Holden?" Taylor questioned, shaking her head. "I guess I can only be glad Amanda didn't discover you standing over Thelma's lifeless body, or I'd be in jail by now. Or don't you always let somebody else take the fall for you?"

Holden stopped dead on the sand, as did Taylor, for he had grabbed her by the elbow, swinging her around in front of him. "Now look, Taylor—" he began angrily, then let out his breath in a rush. "Damn it, you're right. I screwed up. I screwed up big time. First, by listening to Sid—and I'm not blaming any of this on Sid, so don't look at me that way, okay? I'm a big boy now, and I could have told Sid to forget the whole thing the moment he told me about his idiot scheme. I didn't. I went along. And that's my fault."

"Where's a microphone when you want one?" Taylor grumbled, scanning the nearly empty beach. "No cameras, no reporters. Damn. Maybe you'll be willing to repeat that confession when Rich Newsome shows up for a rematch? I mean, this should be recorded for posterity—Holden Masters admitting to doing something wrong. Something lamebrained, even. Dumb. Really, *really* stupid human trick. Yup, the great wonder man goofed, slipped up, royally stuck his foot in it—"

"Oh, shut up," Holden breathed, pulling her hard against him, feeling her slim, spandex-clad body touching him knee to chest before he silenced her sarcastic teasing with his mouth.

She tasted of summer mornings, of salt, of sea air, of the good, clean sweat of healthful exercise. She tasted of sex, of want, of need—and he crushed her mouth against his, eased it open with his eager tongue, plunged the depths of her fueled by a need so strong, so startling, he shook with it.

He felt her arms slide around his back, hungrily kneading his muscles, fluidly running along his spine; felt her eager acquiescence as he slid one bare, muscled leg between hers, pushing against her, feeling her rubbing against him.

It was as if the world had blown apart, and they were the only two people spared—safe on a small, sandy island within a maelstrom of howling winds and clapping thunder. She was everything he had thought she'd be, everything he'd hoped from the first moment he'd laid eyes on her.

And more.

So much more.

So much more that warning bells went off in his head and he found himself putting his hands on her shoulders, easing her away from him. He looked beyond her, to the path they'd taken to come down to the beach, and saw two newspaper photographers greedily snapping pictures.

"Good girl, Taylor. That ought to satisfy them for a while," he commented as nonchalantly as he could, motioning toward their audience.

Taylor shook her head, obviously confused, still caught up in the moment, then turned and looked at the photographers—and back at Holden. "You *bastard,*" she grated from between clenched teeth, her fingertips digging into his back.

He held her where she was, so that she wouldn't run off, so that she wouldn't hit him. "You agreed to go along with the sham, Taylor," he reminded her, hating himself even as he protected himself from the shattering memory of her kiss, remembering that he had no plans to ever, *ever* fall for that age-old fantasy of believing in anything so transient as "true love," which is what his mother had called each and every one of her "forever" marriages. "Relax, it won't happen again."

"And you can bet your Super Bowl ring on that one, Holden Masters," Taylor told him angrily, roughly pulling free of his hold. "When do you plan to leave for the casinos? I might as well go along for the ride, because there's no way in hell I'm touching you again today, therapy or no therapy."

"We'll go after lunch," he told her quickly, before she could run off the beach without him, and fell in behind her as he jogged back to the condo, back to his room—where he lay down on his bed and spent fifteen minutes calling himself every rotten name Taylor had missed.

TAYLOR ACTUALLY WENT so far as to begin packing her luggage, intent on leaving Ocean City and Holden Masters far behind her, before she gave it up as a bad job and sat down on her bed, mumbling aloud, "How did a nice girl like you get mixed up in a mess like this?" just as Tiffany came into the room without knocking.

"I'm bummed," the younger woman announced baldly, pouting as she lifted Taylor's half-filled duffel from the bed, dropped it on the floor, then collapsed on her back on the mattress, looking up at the ceiling. "I mean, totally bummed. Holden says Lance can't come with us. He says he's weird." Tiffany lifted her head an inch off the mattress—the head now framed by hair nearly the same shade as the exterior of the condo—and looked at Taylor, her eyes wide.

"Can you believe that? *Weird?* Lance is *not* weird. He wouldn't think of, like, piercing his tongue, for one thing. Herbie did, though—and Daddykins never even said boo to him the night he came to one of our pool parties and got a nacho chip stuck in it."

"He got a nacho chip stuck in the pool?" Taylor asked, grinning, then shook her head. Proper English, as well as sarcasm, were both totally wasted on Tiffany. "Anyway, that's too bad, Tiff. But you can spend one day away from Lance, can't you?"

The girl rolled her eyes. "Of *course* I can, Taylor, although he'll be, like, totally lost without me. But if I pout, Holden will give me more money for the shops. Jeez, don't you know *anything?*"

"Apparently not," Taylor said, pulling a sweatshirt out from beneath Tiffany's sprawled body, folding it and replacing it in the open drawer. "Did you know Amanda Price is coming with us?" Now, why on earth did she mention that? Taylor shook her head, angry with herself. "Not that it matters, of course."

Tiffany levered herself up on her elbows, an unholy grin splitting her deeply red painted mouth. "Oh-oh—trouble in paradise? *Already?* Well, relax. Holden is crazy about you. It's just that he's always nice to everyone and doesn't want Amanda to feel left out." She dropped back against the mattress, reassuming her self-pitying, martyred pout. "Although he sure hasn't been nice to Lance. Called him a dork.'' She pulled a face. ''Yeah, right. Like anyone says *dork* anymore.''

Taylor turned away, not wanting Tiffany to see her smile. ''What are you going to wear to the casinos, Tiff?'' she asked, hoping to change the subject. ''I thought I'd wear my denim skirt and a knit top.''

''Sounds good,'' Tiffany agreed, sitting up again— the child had more energy than a two-year-old on a sugar high. ''We're going to the Taj Mahal, you know. I asked. The limo is coming at one o'clock.''

''The *limo?*''

''Of course,'' Tiffany answered calmly, while Taylor shook her head, knowing the last time she'd ridden in a limousine was for her high-school prom— and then, three couples had chipped in to hire the thing, so they'd ended up crammed into it like sardines.

''Holden has to take precautions, you know,'' Tiffany explained. ''Be happy he doesn't have bodyguards crawling all over him like Daddykins. Not that he probably won't be sending a bunch of them here any minute now, since Woody and I are in the newspapers this morning. It's *such* a pain! Holden has even asked Lance's last name. I think he's having him checked out on orders from Daddykins. I tell you, I'm *suffocating!*''

Taylor looked into the mirror, saw that her mouth was hanging open and quickly shut it. It had never occurred to her—she hadn't given Tiffany and

Woody's father's fame a second thought, just as she hadn't considered Holden's fame. Until the cameras had shown up, of course. Until those girls had drooled all over him on the beach. Then it had sort of become impossible to miss. But living in the limelight, the spotlight, day after day, year in year out? It had to be terrible!

"I don't think I like this," she said aloud, forgetting Tiffany's presence.

"What's to like?" the younger woman responded as if Taylor's words had been directed at her. "Fame is a royal pain. I think that's why Holden is so crazy about you. You're like Thelma—you don't care who he is. Now, Amanda—well, do you think she'd be hanging around if Holden was a plumber?" She rolled her eyes comically. "Duh! I don't *think* so!"

Tiffany stood up, slapping her hands against her thighs. "Well, I'm outta here. I have to go break the bad news to Lance. He'll be totally crushed, of course, which I consider wonderful. It shows how much he loves me. Oh, and Taylor? If you happen to leave the casino for a while...you know, to walk around a little...and if you see Lance anywhere...well, you'll just keep that little secret to yourself, right?"

"Tiffany, if you're thinking about disobeying Holden, I just want to say that—" Taylor began warningly.

The girl gave her a hug and a kiss. "Thanks, Taylor. You're such a brick! I knew you'd understand!" she exclaimed, then skipped out of the room like a petite green beach ball, all bright and bouncy and full of fun.

Leaving Taylor to wonder yet again how a nice girl like her had ever ended up in a mess like this....

7

IT WAS THE SENIOR PROM all over again.

There has to be a joke in here somewhere, Taylor thought as she held on to the jump seat as the limousine zoomed over the speed bumps in the private roadway leading to the casino. *How many idiots does it take to fill a limousine?* was the first thing that came to mind, although she couldn't seem to come up with a punch line.

Woody and Tiffany were in the limousine, of course, squabbling between themselves like much younger children and generally having themselves a high old time while anticipating an even better one.

And there was also Amanda Price, who had spread out her full skirts on the deep navy velvet seat beside Holden, staking out her territory and leaving no room for Taylor. Or so Amanda must have thought before Thelma Helper—dressed in her "gambling clothes," which included lots of faux-gold leather and polyester, along with a smidgen of fringe—crowded in right after the model and plunked herself down between the two of them.

Which was, or so Taylor told herself, why she didn't mind sitting in the jump seat. In fact, as it gave her a marvelously clear view of Amanda's less than glamorously puckered mouth as Thelma explained the marvel of having her soap opera taped on the VCR while she was gone, the whole experience was rather making her day.

Amanda tried, without notable success, to steer the conversation to friends and experiences she and Holden had shared—and Taylor obviously had not. But Thelma, bless her, kept interrupting—mention of the late, lamented Sam sprinkling the conversation at regular intervals, along with demands the chauffeur take a small detour to the town of Margate to show everyone Lucy the Elephant, a local display—and giving a running commentary on each small town they passed through, its history and its premier ice-cream parlors.

She was just beginning to run down when they entered Atlantic City, at which time she heaved herself forward, knocked on the tinted glass separating them from the driver and yelled at him to stay in the left lane so as not to get stuck behind one of the shuttle buses.

"I think he probably knows that, Thelma," Holden told her politely. "I hired him through the hotel, and he makes runs up here all day long."

"Which explains why he didn't have the correct change at the tollbooth heading out of Ocean City, I suppose,'' Thelma answered with a sniff, then broke into a wide grin as she saw the casinos. "Oh, what fun! Here now, Ms. Price, stop sitting on my bag of quarters."

Amanda, who had already complained—twice—about the plastic bag of loose quarters Thelma had jammed down beside her on the seat, merely lifted her chin and looked disdainfully away.

Taylor decided to treat Thelma to a triple scoop hot fudge sundae the first chance she got.

"Now, when we get inside, Woody," Thelma went on undaunted, zealously explaining casino economy to the son of a multimillionaire, "the first thing you have to do is go get one of those personalized cards for the slot machines. You stick it in each slot machine as you play, and then they send you a voucher for cash or food the next time you come back. I eat free all the time."

"And it only costs you how much in quarters lost to the slot machines?" Holden asked, smiling at Taylor.

"Oh, pish! You're just like Sam," Thelma complained, reaching into the hip pack she had strapped to her waist and pulling out a long, neon yellow strap to which was attached a ring holding a half-dozen plastic cards the size of credit cards. The strap was also plastic and curled like a stretchable telephone cord so she could extend it to reach the slot in the machine. Thelma looped the strap around her neck like a necklace, then began shuffling through the cards until she found the one from the Taj Mahal. "Here it is! See, Woody? I've got one for each casino. You might want to think about stringing yours around your neck, too. Keeps you from losing it."

"Uh-huh," Woody said noncommittally, then winked at Taylor, who did her best not to laugh.

"Do you have a leather visor, too, Thelma? In case you want to play poker, you understand."

"Not funny, Mr. Masters," Thelma scolded. "This is serious business, you know. Real serious. And don't forget the buffet. All you can eat, real cheap. Woody—you listening to me, sonny boy? This is your education."

"Uh-huh," Woody said again, and Taylor recalled the thickness of the young man's wallet as he'd stuffed it into his shorts pocket. "I'll remember. But, Thelma—don't you want to go to dinner with us? Holden's already made reservations. He's taking us to the steak house in the casino."

Thelma dismissed that offer with a wave of both hands. "Steak-schmake." She then turned to wink at Holden. "Poor boy, he has *so* much to learn! Before-dinner drinks. Appetizers. Dessert. People waiting on you hand and foot. That could take hours. I don't want to lose time on the floor. Ah, here we are. Look out, Mr. Masters—from here on in, it's every man for himself! Besides, I'm dying for a cigarette, now that I'll be away from Miss 'Good God, I'm allergic!''' she told him, already climbing over him and opening the door, although she did spare a backward glance at Amanda, who had refused to allow her to smoke in the limousine. "We meet right back here at ten, right?" she asked, then scooted out without waiting for an answer.

"Holden, I cannot understand the reason behind bringing that ridiculous woman with us," Amanda said, brushing down her designer skirt. "Those terrible cigarettes—and all that ridiculous red lipstick. Honestly, I'm glad she's gone. It's embarrassing to be seen with her. She would have, I'm sure, felt much more at home on a bus, or some such thing."

"Well, I like her, and so does Holden. We all do," Woody said firmly, glaring at the supermodel. "Besides, I can't understand the reason behind bringing *you* along. Don't you know you're yesterday's news?"

"Woodstock," Holden growled warningly, looking to Taylor as if for help. She didn't give him any.

Why, she might not even toss Holden a marshmallow if he were in the middle of a burning building.

Hand him a wet blotter if he were crawling through a desert.

Pass him a feather if he were falling out of an airplane.

She might, if he were starving, peel a hard-boiled egg and toss him the shell.

Maybe.

But she wasn't going to help him now.

No sir-ree. Uh-uh. Nope. Not her. Not right now. Not after what he said and did this morning on the beach. And maybe, just maybe, because he *had* brought Amanda along this afternoon.

"Woody, don't be a jerk," Tiffany snapped, then smiled at the driver as he offered her his hand and hopped lightly to the pavement in front of the casino, at which time she turned in a full circle, taking in the sight of multicolored minarets high above her. "Holy cow! We're deep into tacky here, aren't we? Kewl!"

Taylor inclined her head to Holden as he motioned for her and Amanda to precede him out of the limousine, and within less than a minute, five people had called out, "Isn't that him? Holden Masters? Hey—number 8! How's it going? You coming back to the team?"

Holden smiled and joked, signing more than a few autographs, then escorted his small party inside, where they were met by one of the casino staff, who promised them they were very, very welcome indeed.

"You ever get sick of this?" Taylor asked out of the corner of her mouth as Holden held out his right arm to her—while holding out his left to Amanda, who was openly preening at all the commotion.

"It comes with the territory, Taylor," he answered, then smiled as someone took his picture. "But people leave you alone after a while, honest.

Just keep smiling for now, okay? It's only a little attention.''

And it was impossible to escape that attention. Holden was tall and broad and handsome—one of those naturally bigger-than-life sort of people no one could ignore—and his face graced everything from television commercials to cereal boxes. He was, as they said in the bleachers, "the man."

With the tall, willowy, professionally gorgeous Amanda Price on his arm—and some little nobody on his other one—Holden Masters made quite an entrance. Having the beachboy handsome Woodstock LeGrand and the exotic, giggling, green-haired Tiffany LeGrand also in tow certainly didn't make them any more inconspicuous, and it took a good ten minutes to get through the lobby and into the casino.

Holden stopped at the entrance and turned to Tiffany. "You know you can't come in here, right? I mean, we went all over this at home, remember?"

Tiffany clearly wasn't listening. She stood just at the entrance, just beyond the uniformed guard, gnawing on the nail of her baby finger, going up on tiptoe as she peered into the cavernous room that was alive with people, blinking lights and the sound of ringing bells. "Damn," she mouthed quietly, then looked toward the machines that were closest to the doors, assessing them.

And then she smiled. She reached into her small purse and pulled out two fifty-dollar bills, pressing them into her brother's outstretched hand. ''That one, Woody. That one, right over there—with all the red, white and blue sevens in it. Do that one.''

''Excuse me, miss,'' the guard began, looking at Tiffany's sandal-clad feet, which were very close to standing on the ''wrong'' carpet. ''Do you have proof of age?''

Tiffany rolled her eyes. ''Would I be standing here if I had proof of age?'' she asked before pushing Woody into the casino.

''I don't think he can gamble for you, miss,'' the guard began, only to have Holden cut him off.

''She was just holding his money for him,'' Holden explained quickly. ''She won't try to go onto the floor, I promise.''

The guard looked Holden up and down, then nodded. ''You're Holden Masters, aren't you? You look better with the mustache, you know,'' he said, clearly not impressed. ''Okay, I'll know who to go after if she tries any tricks. Can't let underage kids in here. Just can't.''

''I understand completely,'' Holden said, then followed Woody into the casino, calling over his shoulder to Tiffany to ''stay'' and ''mind.'' She stuck out her tongue at him, but did as he said.

''I imagine that guard sees a lot of celebrities in the course of his job,'' Taylor offered as they stood behind Woody, watching him play off the credits from the hundred dollars he had fed into the machine's bill changer. "You're right, Holden, the attention only lasts for a little while. Thank goodness. I was beginning to understand what a goldfish feels like. Holden—Woody's playing three coins at a time, and this is a dollar machine! That's three dollars every time you pull on that handle. Does Tiffany have any idea just how fast one hundred dollars can disappear into one of these things?"

"Oh, yeah," Woody said calmly, his eyes on the rotating sevens. "We've done this before, lots of times, when we travel with Dad. But let me tell you— she's got a real eye for this stuff. Never misses. It's like she's got some kind of radar, you know?" As if to prove Woody correct, the machine locked in with three lovely sevens straight across the line, and bells and whistles and lights signaled that Woody had hit a jackpot. *"Yes!"* he exclaimed, running out of the casino to slap high fives with Tiffany. He ran back in to grin at Taylor. "Told ya. Never misses. Now she'll let us alone and go shopping."

Taylor stared at the machine, bug-eyed, checking the lines, reading the payoff amounts. Three sevens all in a row, red, white and blue, on the third payline. Woody had won the grand jackpot. Ten thousand dollars! Ten—count 'em—*thousand* dollars!

"I don't believe it," she mumbled under her breath. "Guess that's the old rule of 'them that has,' huh?" she asked, turning to Holden.

"Believe it or not, Taylor," he answered, not smiling, "I'd still call the two of them underprivileged children, if that saying is still in style."

Taylor closed her eyes a moment, knowing exactly what Holden meant. Benevolent neglect would be the most flattering term she could come up with to describe Peter LeGrand's parenting style. How lucky for Woody and Tiffany that they had Holden in their lives.

A half hour later, after Woody had had his picture taken next to the machine—and met his very own IRS agent—Tiffany was off to the second-floor shops with Amanda in tow, and Taylor and Holden were free to walk around the casino. Woody, however, had already found the roulette table and, or so he promised, would be staying right there until it was time to go to dinner, if anyone wanted to find him.

Nobody did. Or at least Taylor found herself to be curiously happy to finally be away from everyone and alone with Holden, who showed no inclination to place a single bet anywhere. Not that she'd tell *him* that she was pleased to be in his company. So they just walked along, looking at the millions of lights, the thousands of people, and not saying much of anything.

She thought she should feel awkward, being alone with him after what had happened on the beach only that morning, but she didn't. She didn't feel awkward and she was no longer angry. She felt happy and relaxed, and curiously proud of how *normal* he seemed in the midst of all his fame, all the silly craziness of having Woody and Tiffany—and even Thelma—in his life.

"You want to put a few coins through a machine?" Holden asked at last, as they reached an exit at the other side of the large casino.

She smiled and shook her head. "There's no way I could even hope to top what Woody and Tiffany did. Wait until Thelma hears what happened. She'll want Tiffany to come back here with her every day for the rest of the summer."

Holden shook his head. "That won't happen. Tiff bores easily, which is my only hope where Lance is concerned. If only Amanda would take the hint."

Taylor enjoyed his discomfort. "That's what happens when you're seen everywhere together for nearly six months. A girl starts believing you really like her, although I have to admit I'm a little surprised she hasn't simply slapped your face and gone away, because you've really thrown her a curve—if I might use a baseball analogy to a football man. She must really be smitten. Not that I'm in any danger of succumbing to the Masters charm myself, mind you. It would be pretty difficult to misunderstand the reason for our so-called engagement."

Shut up, she told herself, snapping her teeth together. *You're babbling like the village idiot! Next you'll be telling him how you've noticed that Aman-*

da's mouth doesn't move when she talks, probably because she's trying not to get wrinkles.

Holden looked at her, rather strangely, she thought, then said, "Speaking of which, let's head upstairs to the jewelry store, all right? There's still the matter of a ring, remember?"

Taylor stopped in her tracks, refusing to budge, all thoughts of Amanda Price and her immovable mouth deserting her. "No," she said succinctly. "I know I've gone along with everything else—and the moment I figure out why I have, I'll be a happy woman—but I draw the line at a ring, just as I told you this morning. So, thank you, but no."

Holden took on a long-suffering expression, as if accustomed to women turning down his offers of jewelry, as if he had expected this reluctance, believing it was now his job to convince her to do what she wanted to do all along—which would be to take the diamonds and run. "Taylor, it's just a piece of jewelry. A gift between friends. Come on, I want to give you a present."

"I said no," Taylor repeated, feeling mulish, more than mulish. Feeling suddenly weepy. Didn't he have any idea what he was asking of her? A ring was more than some gold, a cold stone, a magnificent gesture that might be worth a small fortune to most everyone else but was no more than the cost of one product endorsement television commercial to him. A ring was a commitment, a symbol, a promise. It wasn't a prop. Not that she could tell him that.

Holden sighed. "Taylor..."

Taylor's temper flared, mostly because she felt tears stinging at the backs of her eyes and resented how Holden's offhand, conventional gesture had instigated them. "Look, Holden, what part of *no* can't you understand? My mother took off her engagement ring once—in church, to let Dad slip a wedding ring on her finger. Oh, she has it cleaned once in a while, but that's it. Those rings have been on her finger so long her finger has shrunk around them, so that they twist sometimes. I know it's only a stone to you, only a superstition, a meaningless symbol, a quirk, even a bit of propaganda put out by jewelers trying to make a buck—whatever you want to call it— but, damn it, Holden, not to me! Not to me."

He reached up and scratched behind his ear, looking confused and adorably handsome. For a smart man, he certainly had a lot to learn about women and their vulnerable hearts. And she wondered why nothing in his life had ever taught him. "All right, Taylor. No diamonds. No traditional engagement ring."

Out of the corner of her eye, Taylor thought she saw Lance creeping toward the lobby. No, she *did* see Lance creeping toward the lobby. *Oh, brother, here we go,* she silently groaned, barely paying attention to Holden—although she was pretty sure he'd agreed not to buy her diamonds. She let out her breath in a grateful sigh. "Thank you."

"You're welcome. So it's settled. We'll get you a ruby one. Or one of those green stones. I don't care—pick a color," he said, taking hold of her hand and pulling her along to the escalator, leaving her no choice but to hop on the moving metal stairs and hang on for dear life—all while peeking back to where Lance had been and to where he wasn't anymore.

TAYLOR ANGEL WAS the most exasperating woman he'd ever met!

She'd come along with him until he'd located the jewelry store, his warning grip on her hand not leaving her much choice, but she had refused to try on any of the rings he pointed out to her in the glass cases.

"Pick one," Holden had told her, ordered her, asked her, *pleaded* with her each time the salesperson left to wait on another customer. "For the love of heaven, just close your eyes and pick one."

She avoided his eyes as she had done for the past twenty minutes. "Why?"

He closed his own eyes a moment, counting to ten. "Because everyone in the world expects you to have an engagement ring."

Now she looked at him. Coolly. Levelly. "No. I'd need a better reason than that."

"All right." He searched his brain for logical reasons, not wanting to tell her that, for some absolutely unfathomable reason, he really did want to give her a present.

A present that he would see every day. A present that would be a gesture, more than a gesture. A mark of ownership? No. Couldn't be that.

He struggled to find something to say and improvised, "Because Amanda won't go away until she has some sort of proof that this engagement is real, okay? Tact, she doesn't understand. Manners, she doesn't understand. Jewelry, the lady understands."

Taylor's left eyebrow lifted a fraction. "No."

He tried another avenue. "Woody wants you to have a ring."

"Say that one again."

Ah, progress! He should have thought of this sooner—she *liked* Woody. "I said, Woody asked if I had gotten you a ring yet. He expects it of me, of us."

"*Woody* wants me to have a ring. Marvelous." She turned and walked down the long line of glass-topped cases, trailing her fingers along the edge.

He went after her, feeling stupid and clumsy, and not a little angry. "And Tiffany mentioned it to me this morning. Called me a slacker."

She kept moving. "*Tiffany* wants me to have a ring. Double marvelous. And has Thelma gotten a vote, or were two opinions enough for you?"

Holden threw up his hands in defeat. "All right, all right! *I* want you to have a ring. *I* think it would be a good idea. *I* owe you something for this favor you're doing me, damn it.''

"You *owe* me? Again, thanks but no thanks. You were close for a minute there, Holden, old sport, but no cigar. Care to try again?''

He was getting desperate. "Taylor, you'll pick out a ring now, or I'm going to kiss you," he all but growled. "I'm going to kiss you long. I'm going to kiss you hard. I'm going to kiss you in front of all these people until your toes curl in your shoes.''

Her eyes went wide as she looked up at him. "You wouldn't dare.''

He lowered his face to within an inch of hers and grinned. "Try me.''

She hesitated only a few seconds, then blurted out quickly, "I'll take that one—over there, in the second case. Third one from the left, fourth row. The sapphire with the diamond baguettes. Gold setting. And probably worth a king's ransom in markup. Happy now?''

"Delighted!'' And then he kissed her anyway. Because she was the most exasperating woman he'd ever met.

8

TAYLOR EXCUSED HERSELF once she and Holden were back on the casino floor, mumbling something about needing to powder her nose, and immediately went off in search of Lance—and Tiffany. Because where she found one, she would be sure to find the other.

She should have known Tiffany hadn't sought out Amanda Price's company because she trusted the woman's fashion sense. Fashion, to Tiffany, meant something highly outrageous and startling. To Amanda, it meant fabulously expensive and impressive.

And Amanda couldn't care less about Tiffany or about anyone, probably, other than herself. It was a harsh judgment and one Taylor berated herself for making, but she had good reasons not to like the supermodel.

None of them, however, that she was ready to admit to herself. Not now, with Holden's "engagement" ring on her finger.

Taylor searched a few minutes, then stopped dead, feeling she was in the middle of an endless maze. Had someone told her that the Taj Mahal was the largest casino in Atlantic City? Even if it wasn't true, she was more than ready to believe it as she searched the casino aisles, careful to stay out of sight of the roulette tables, where Holden had gone to join Woody.

Why did she feel so responsible for Tiffany, for Woody, even for Holden, for Pete's sake? Why was she worried about them? It wasn't as if any of them were more than transitory figures in her life, right? It wasn't as if she really *cared.* . . .

"Where *are* you?" she muttered under her breath, giving the lie to her self-protective thoughts as she sought vainly for the sight of lime green hair.

She'd kill Tiffany if she'd tried to get onto the casino floor. Absolutely, positively *kill* her. Didn't Holden have enough trouble without adding a sister arrested for underage gambling to the list?

Yet, Taylor was convinced that underage gambling was just what Tiffany had in mind. What other mischief could she be up to? Mischief that included Lance. Mischief that excluded letting anyone else in on her plans?

Just as she was about to abandon the casino floor and check out the shops again, Taylor caught sight of Thelma Helper out of the corner of her eye. The woman was sitting in front of a quarter machine, her eyes glazed as if she had been staring at the twirling tumblers for hours—which she probably had.

"Thelma!" she exclaimed, coming up behind the housekeeper so suddenly that Thelma's body jerked as if she had been shot, a movement that succeeded in pulling her gambling card out of its slot as the yellow neon strap slapped back, hitting her in the face.

"Don't *do* that, child!" Thelma scolded, rubbing at her stinging nose. "Can't you see that I'm concentrating? I'm up twenty dollars, would you believe it?"

"I'm sorry, Thelma," Taylor apologized quickly, then just as quickly added, "for startling you, I mean. Congratulations on your win. It's wonderful, really. Um . . . have you see Tiffany?"

Thelma replaced the card in its slot, fed three more quarters into the machine and pulled the handle. "I haven't left this machine since I got here. Of course I didn't see Tiffany."

The reels spun, with no winner. Thelma fed the hungry machine three more quarters. "Why? What did she do—buy out the shoe store? That child has more money than sense, you know. You'll be real good for her, Taylor, once you convince Mr. Masters that this should be more real engagement than dumb publicity stunt—and don't bother telling me that it isn't, because I wasn't born yesterday. You know, teach the child a little of what life is really about." A bell rang once and the machine spit out some coins. "Hot damn! Two quarters!"

"But you put in three, Thelma," Taylor remarked, then realized the woman wasn't listening to her. She was too busy sliding three more coins into the slot.

Turning away and knowing she could never tell Thelma how Tiffany had hit the jackpot, Taylor retraced her steps to the first-floor shops, poking her head into the ice-cream parlor and the gift store before giving in to the impulse to go out onto the boardwalk for a little fresh air. Maybe it would clear her head—if anything could. She felt as if she'd been caught up in Thelma's soap or some other outlandish plot.

All the millions of lights, mirrors and overdone glamour of the Taj Mahal, combined with the clanging bells and the sound of coins dropping into metal trays, had taken their toll on Taylor's nerves—not to mention the addition of the guilty weight of the ring now on her third finger, left hand. She needed to ground herself, center herself again, and to remember that this was all a dream, that Cinderella turned back into a serving girl at midnight.

As she walked along, she took three deep breaths of the salty summer air, then wrinkled her nose at the smell of greasy hamburgers from a nearby storefront wafting by on a breeze. The boardwalk in Atlantic City was a far cry from the one in Ocean City—wider, seedier and a lot more crowded at this late-afternoon hour. She had to step back quickly to avoid an electric tram carrying gamblers from one casino to another, then nearly had her ankle clipped by one of the bicycle chairs she could remember riding in as a child, when her parents had brought her to the seashore.

Looking both ways as if ready to cross a Manhattan street at rush hour, she made for the railing and the view of the sand and ocean that awaited her. Gulls screamed and laughed overhead, dive-bombing a small child trying to protect a paper cup full of French fries, and Taylor laughed at the sight before a flash of green hair caught her eye at last.

Tiffany.

And Lance, stuck to her like a tall, painfully thin tube of glue.

They were turning off the boardwalk, going down a ramp onto a side street not half a block from where Taylor was standing—or where she had been standing until she'd seen the pair of teenagers. She broke into a jog, deftly darting between pedestrians, boardwalk musicians, bicycle chairs and panhandlers, following where the green hair led while carefully remaining out of sight so they wouldn't see her before she could catch up to them.

The couple walked the length of two long city blocks before turning again onto one of the narrow cross streets, and Taylor stopped at the corner, poking her head around cautiously, trying to see where they were heading.

But they were gone. Disappeared like a magician in a puff of smoke.

Taylor fought the urge to go back to the casino and locate Holden, but realized that would take too long—and heaven only knew what mischief Tiffany could get herself into in the meantime.

She turned the corner, took a deep breath and began looking into the front windows of the rather seedy shops that lined the street. Pawnshops. Check-cashing storefronts. A used-clothing store. The flip side of all the lights and glamour on the other end of the street.

"I'm going to murder that child when I find her," Taylor muttered under her breath as a man carrying a brown paper bag—and drinking from the bottle concealed inside it as he walked toward her—commented on how he'd like to show her a "good time." She gritted her teeth, used her thumb to twist the ring so that its jewels were facing her palm and quickly walked on, looking into the dirty front window of yet another narrow shop.

And there they were. Tiffany and Lance. Sitting in a dingy room, looking toward the dingier curtain that appeared to serve as a divider to another room.

Taylor stepped back and looked up at the front of the building to read the sign nailed to the crumbling brick. *Lily's Tattoo Emporium.*

Taylor's hands drew into fists as she once more forgot that she was *not* involved with Holden Masters and his family. "Oh, yeah. I'm *definitely* going to kill her, or at least maim her. Badly!" she pronounced angrily, then pushed open the door to the tattoo parlor, sending the tin bell above the door to tinkling and two young heads to turning in her direction.

"Hey, Tiff, *kewl.* Your brother's girl is getting a tattoo, too," Lance said, nodding his head like one of those loose-headed dog statues bobbing along in the rear window of a pickup truck. "Think she'll put Hayden's name on her butt?"

"That's *Holden,* you idiot. Holden Masters, best quarterback in the history of the—oh, forget it! You just don't get beyond Hootie and the Blowfish, do you, Lance?" Tiffany responded, hopping to her feet even as she pinned a bright smile on her face. "Taylor! Boy, talk about coincidences! What are you doing here?"

"What else, Tiff? I'm waiting for a bus," Taylor answered, wincing as she heard the buzz of a tattoo needle from behind the curtain. "You're coming with me, Tiffany. *Now!*"

Tiffany's pretty young face turned mulish as she sat down again, crossing her arms across her chest. "No. I'm not. I'm getting a tattoo. Lance's name—with a *lance* through it. Get it? Isn't that just the raddest thing you ever heard? A Lance and a lance. On my butt!"

Lance's head bobbed again. "Yeah. And I'm getting a Tiffany—with a . . . with a—Tiff? What am I getting with my tattoo?"

"Blood poisoning?" Taylor offered affably, still feeling in control of the situation. After all, these were only kids. Surely she could control two silly young kids. Or could she? "Tiffany—forget it, okay? I'd list all the reasons you don't want a tattoo, but we don't have three hours. Holden's going to be sending out a search party for the both of us soon."

Mulish did not begin to describe the look on Tiffany's face now. Determined didn't even come close. Resolute? Resolved? Obstinate? Adamant? *Immovable.* Yes, immovable. That would be the one Taylor would pick. But if Taylor had her way, Tiffany LeGrand's *immovable* was going to become mobile, and in a hurry.

She counted to three in her head, then landed on a plan. "All right, Tiffany," Taylor said, walking over to a large wall chart depicting some of the available "art" Lily the Tattoo Artist offered to her patrons. "Have it your way. Get Lance's name on your butt. I think it's cute—in a juvenile, stupid-stunt sort of way."

"You do? Tiffany asked, walking over to stand beside Taylor, who was still looking at the displayed artwork and actually becoming rather fascinated by the drawing of an American eagle with at least a three-foot wingspread. *Where would you put that?* she wondered, then brought herself back to attention.

"Yes, Tiffany, I do. After all, what more personal expression of affection can there be than to have someone's name burned into your rear end for all time? And the pain? Why, the pain and possible infection—that's dedication, Tiffany. Real dedication!''

"Oh, yeah? My friend, Daphne, got a rose on her ankle. In Malibu. She said it didn't hurt a bit. Daphne wouldn't lie to me.''

"Of course not.'' Taylor leaned forward, tracing a finger over the drawing of a gorilla wearing a smiley face. "See this, Tiffany? It's kind of like connect the dots—in a flesh-searing sort of way. The needle burns into the skin—burn, burn, burn—and before you know it, you've got a whole line. Let's see. Lance. Five letters. You aren't getting capitals, are you? They'd take more dots, you know. And then there's the lance. About two hundred dots in a lance, don't you think?'' She made a face. "Too bad his name isn't Ed. Shorter, you know. Fewer dots.''

"Daphne said it didn't hurt,'' Tiffany repeated, although she was now pressing a fingertip against the picture of a skull, counting dots.

"Once the swelling goes down, why, I can't see how it could. If it doesn't get infected, of course,'' Taylor said blandly.

At that moment, a leather-vest-and-jeans-clad mountain of a man came out from behind the curtain—his beefy arms nearly all blue from dozens of tattoos—and growled out, "Next?''

Tiffany's eyes became as round as saucers.

"Where's Lily?" Lance asked, looking rather anemic under his tan as he slowly shrank back in the cracked-vinyl chair.

"I'm Lily," the man mountain said sniffing, then wiping his nose with his index finger. "Nathaniel Jerome Lily. You got a problem with that, sonny?"

"Actually, Mr. Lily, I think we've just remembered a previous engagement," Taylor put in helpfully, sending up a silent thank-you for Whoever had whispered in her ear that her best chance of talking Tiffany out of a tattoo was not to lay down rules, but just "go with the flow." With maybe just a small *nudge* in the direction of sanity.

"Um, yeah—*yeah*," Lance said quickly, nearly tripping over his own feet as he stood up and grabbed onto Tiffany's elbow. "That's it. A previous engagement. Isn't that right, Tiff?"

"You're *afraid!*" she countered contemptuously, sneering. For a moment, a remarkably queasy moment, Taylor thought Tiffany was going to go through with it, just to show Lance who was the stronger of the two of them, but then the girl huffed and said, "Just remember, Lance. *I* would have done it for *you.*"

They were outside on the cracked pavement within moments, Taylor leading the way back to the boardwalk. "Lance, you're going back to Ocean City—*now*. How did you get here?"

"Bus," he said, obviously still smarting over his poor showing as a man who would give his all—or at least a portion of his backside—for the woman he loved.

"Very well, the bus it is. Happy trails, bucko," Taylor said firmly, sending him on his way as they stood outside the doors to the casino once more. "Say goodbye, Lance."

"Goodbye, Tiff," he mumbled sheepishly, putting his hands in his pockets, his chin on his chest, and wandering away like a lost Labrador. He turned back to look longingly at Tiffany. "See ya."

"Oh, for pity's sake!" Taylor exclaimed, calling him back. "Look," she said, sighing. "If I say *I* ran into Lance by accident and asked him to join us, do you suppose you could behave yourself for the rest of the day? Tiffany? I'm talking to you."

"You're not my mother, you know," Tiffany stated, looking mulish again. And then she smiled. "This is like television. 'The Brady Bunch.' The kids get into trouble, and the stepmother bails them out. Did I learn a lesson along the way? I think I'm supposed to learn a lesson along the way."

Taylor rolled her eyes, knowing she was rapidly going down for the count—getting *way* too involved with Holden and his family. "I think I'm the one who learned a lesson, Tiffany," she said as Lance held open the door. He probably would have thrown his body down over a mud puddle for them, if there had been a mud puddle in the casino lobby. "And that lesson is—well, damn. I don't know what the lesson is."

Tiffany went up on tiptoe and planted a kiss on Taylor's cheek. "Thanks, Taylor. Thanks a lot. Holden made a good choice."

Don't get involved, Taylor's brain screamed at her as she watched Tiffany and Lance go off to the ice-cream parlor for sundaes. *That's the lesson, Ms. Angel. Don't get involved. Hearts get broken that way, you know....*

THERE WAS AMPLE ROOM in the limousine for Lance, thanks to Amanda's defection. The woman had met an old friend—with older money—at the baccarat tables and deserted what she, even as dense as she was, could see was a rapidly sinking matrimonial ship. Without so much as a goodbye for Taylor or Thelma—who probably had been happy enough to have missed the woman's exit—Amanda Price had walked away with her friend and out of Holden's life.

Holden hadn't bothered to watch her go.

Amanda Price, he thought as he and his family rode through the darkness back to Ocean City. *Good name. You always knew she had one. A "price," that is. All of them did.*

Holden sighed, thinking of Amanda, of all the beautiful, ambitious women who had come and gone in his life for the past eleven years, ever since he'd signed his first pro contract. He barely remembered their names, their faces. All he remembered now was the regret that none of them had been memorable. Different. Unique.

Like Taylor Angel.

He'd never forget her face, her name. He'd never forget how she had coaxed Thelma Helper into joining them for dinner and then listened raptly as the housekeeper had recounted the rollicking weekend she and her Sam had spent at Coney Island a million years ago, riding the coaster and daring each other to take the parachute ride.

He'd never forget how she had talked with Tiffany about Daddykins and Maw-maw, two of the most self-centered, neglectful people this side of fantasy-land, and then steered the conversation to Tiffany's hopes of becoming a genetic engineer. Holden hadn't known Tiffany had even applied to college, let alone been accepted. As a matter of fact, he hadn't realized Tiffany didn't still believe babies were hatched from chicken eggs. No. He wasn't *that* naive. He'd seen the looks his stepsister was giving Lance.

He'd never forget how Taylor had even drawn Lance out, discovering that the boy's parents lived in Manhattan, not two blocks from Sidney Feldon's condo, oddly enough, or that Lance was the son of a New York attorney and had three younger brothers, none of whom had yet to pierce a single body part. His parents obviously had a lot to look forward to.

And Holden would never, ever forget how, all through dinner, Taylor had laughed and made everyone else laugh, and how Woody had looked at her with worshipful eyes and how the young man had confided over dessert that he had been accepted into graduate school, majoring in theater arts. *Woody.* Woodstock LeGrand, he of the surfboards and silly dreams. It was a marvel!

Holden felt humbled, and he felt content. Marvelously content. Nearly domestic. When he wasn't thinking about how to get Taylor into bed with him.

He sat up so swiftly that Woody immediately asked if something was wrong.

"Did you pull one too many slot-machine handles? Does your shoulder hurt?" Taylor inquired, reaching across the seat of the limousine to run her discerning fingers over his deltoid muscle.

"No, no, I'm fine," Holden said as the limousine slowed to a stop outside the Ocean City condo. He rubbed a hand over his face, realizing that he had broken out in a sweat. "I just had a small cramp in my leg. It's gone now. Thelma—it's nearly midnight. You can come in late tomorrow. I'll take everyone up on the boardwalk for breakfast. You want to join us—around nine?"

"You don't hear me complaining, do you?" the housekeeper responded briskly as the others climbed out of the limousine, leaving her room to spread out on the cushioned seat for her solitary ride home. "Do you think anyone would get mad if I had the driver honk the horn a few times before he pulls up in front of my house? Last time I rode in anything this long, I was in the limo behind Sam's hearse. I want to show them how much I've come up in the world.''

"Go for it, Thelma," Holden said with a smile, shaking his head at the woman's obvious glee, then put his hand around Taylor's wrist, holding her in place beside him, even as he tossed the condo keys to Woody. "We're going to take a walk. You two go to bed."

"A walk? At midnight? Well, I suppose so." Taylor shrugged, then fell into step beside him, and Holden felt a rush of relief and of anticipation. "You want to walk on the beach? There's a full moon tonight."

In answer, he slipped his arm around her waist as he guided her across the street, heading for the path through the dunes.

She smiled up at him in the light from a street lamp. "Well, well, Mr. Masters," she teased, obviously referring to his hand at her waist. "Is this what they call a quarterback sneak?"

Holden grinned back at her, remembering their kiss in the jewelry store. She might have been embarrassed, but she hadn't pulled away from him. "A proper call, when all that's needed is short yardage."

"However, if memory serves," Taylor answered, "when you're deep in your own territory, it might be best to drop back ten and punt."

He took a chance. "Am I, Taylor? Deep in my own territory? Or have I passed the twenty and entered the red zone, with a chance to score?"

Taylor tripped over the curbing and would have fallen if Holden hadn't grabbed her, holding her close as they searched each other's face in the dim light. He could feel how tense she was as she leaned into him, hear the tremor in her voice as she murmured quietly, "'Ray, team...."

9

THEY LEFT THEIR SHOES near the path through the dunes and walked barefoot across the sand, neither of them speaking, Holden's arm once more around her waist, Taylor's mind going a million miles a minute.

He was going to make love to her. Either here, on this deserted, moonlit beach, or later, back at the condo. In her room—her ground-floor bedroom. Her secluded, just-in-front-of-the-garage-and-next-to-the-utility-closet bedroom. The room she had chosen because it was so very, very private, cut off from the rest of the condo.

But she hadn't chosen it so that she could entertain a lover.

Especially a six-months-and-you're-out, thanks-it's-been-fun lover.

And so, being a highly sophisticated woman of the world, accustomed to such "I'm man, you're woman, why not?" situations—not!—Taylor immediately began to babble, speaking faster than she could think.

"How do you *stand* having all those people goggling at you wherever you go? Asking for autographs? Coming up to us in the middle of dinner?

Stopping you on the casino floor to compliment your play, or to tell you how you single-handedly blew the Green Bay game? Which you didn't, by the way. That loss was all the coach's fault because he called in the play from the sidelines.''

"Oh? You remember that?''

"Yes. I saw you arguing with him when you immediately called time-out and went roaring toward the sidelines. That's the beauty of watching games on television—they replay all the good stuff. Even *I* could read your lips! Some *French*, Masters! But then, I never could understand the logic in shoving off the ball to a guy five yards in the backfield when you only need two yards for a first down. He was a sitting duck. Reggie White had that poor guy for lunch!''

"Jamal had two cracked ribs after that play. But it was a clean hit.''

Taylor's head was spinning. Holden had rolled up his pants legs and opened his shirt collar. He was so big, so close, and he looked so good, smelled so good. And she knew what was beneath that shirt; had smoothed warm oil over those muscles, felt their supple strength.

"Um, yes, but getting back to what I was saying, or trying to say,'' she blurted out quickly, wishing her palms weren't tingling. "I mean, I don't think I could take all that attention and still keep smiling. And the same with Woody and Tiffany. Because of their fa-

ther, they're always smack in the middle of the spotlight. Do you know that Woody got a kidnap threat
last year in college? Of course you do. Well, like I
said—I don't know how you handle it all with such
grace, such charm.''

"And the occasional punch to the nose, if you remember Rich Newsome," Holden said, easing away
from her as they neared the shoreline and turned to
walk in the shallow water, so that his hand no longer
lay on her waist, but held her own hand in a warm,
comforting squeeze—as if he had sensed her nervousness and was consciously backing off, giving her
room. "But I'm sorry if you were uncomfortable all
day.''

"Oh, no—no!" she hastened to explain. "I liked
it, I did. It was sort of fun. For a while, at least, with
the reporters, those girls goggling at us on the beach.
The attention was rather flattering. Almost funny.
Nobody ever paid any attention to me before. Why,
until today, I probably could have walked stark, staring naked through the Taj Mahal and no one would
have noticed me.''

"Now why do I doubt that?" he questioned her, his
grin lighting his eyes and making them sparkle like
emeralds in the moonlight gliding over the ocean.

Taylor felt her cheeks growing hot and was grateful for the pale, partially concealing light of the
moon. "You know what I mean," she groused, kick-

ing almost viciously at a wavelet breaking on the cool, wet sand just ahead of her.

"I know you're having more than a small problem being a part of this charade I so stupidly got you involved with," he countered. "Which is probably because you're so damned decent, so damned honest— unlike the way I've been for far too long. And I'm not just talking about Sid's smoke screen about my injury or this damn stupid fake engagement. The way I see it, Taylor, I've gotten to be about as real, as genuine, as Tiff's green hair."

She stepped in front of him, putting her hands on his arms, so that he had to stop walking. "You're too hard on yourself, Holden," she told him honestly— a part of her wondering why she wasn't taking the out he had handed her and escaping back to the condo and sanity.

"You're a wonderful person," she continued, digging the pit beneath her feet even deeper with each word. "Really. I've watched how you are with Woody and Tiffany. The way you are with Thelma. Even the way you couldn't just leave Amanda out there to dangle in front of a blood-hungry press, but took her along to Atlantic City—the way you would have kept including her in your plans until she found a way to make a graceful, face-saving exit. You're *not* a fake, Holden. You have genuine feelings for people, genuinely like them. Even fans who ask for your autograph in the middle of the appetizer, then tell you you're rapidly getting past your prime.''

His hands were on her waist once more. ''You're crazy about me, aren't you?'' he teased, lowering his head to begin nuzzling at the taut skin just below her left ear.

''I think I'm just crazy,'' she breathed around the sudden lump in her throat. ''I also think what you're planning next is against the law. At least on a public beach.''

She pushed herself away from him and began walking back toward the path cut into the sand dune, wondering if she was making her escape, or leading him to her bedroom. Either way, she decided she *definitely* had to be crazy.

''Taylor,'' he said, catching up to her, taking hold of her arm just above the elbow as he stood in front of her, his face fairly well lit by the moonlight, his expression deadly serious, deadly earnest. ''You said something a while ago about the two of us being stopped by Amanda in my bedroom the other day just as we were about to go at each other like crazed rabbits. Remember?''

She lowered her head, refusing to look at him, unable to look at him. ''I remember.''

''But it's more than that, isn't it? There's more than just this wild physical attraction. I don't know what it is, but it's there. I feel it. I think you feel it.''

''Yes, I feel it. I won't lie to you.''

"No. You'd never do that, would you? Just as I won't lie to you. The ring on your finger is real, but the reason behind it isn't. We both know that. You're only doing Sid and me a favor, and I'm not the marrying kind, if I can sound like a cliché here. I'm just not. Not that we know each other half well enough to even discuss marriage."

"But you want to make love with me," Taylor said when Holden stopped speaking, probably because his tongue had tied itself into a knot. She could sympathize with the feeling. "Because of our mutual physical attraction. And because we, well, we *like* each other. But because I'm not like Amanda, like all the sophisticated and woman-of-the-world types you've been with, you don't want me to get hurt. Don't want me to start thinking showers and rice and babies. Right?"

He leaned his forehead against hers, and she felt tears burning at the back of her eyes. "Yeah. I guess that just about says it. And it sounds ugly. Damn ugly. And particularly selfish on my part."

Taylor put her hands together and pulled off the ring, then pressed it into Holden's hand. "There. Now nothing's between us. No bargains, no promises, no props, no strings. No possible misunderstandings. Just you and me, and a short walk back to my bedroom. Or did you think you're the only selfish one standing on this beach? I want you, Holden Masters. I really, really want you. I won't ask any-

thing else from you, ever. And I won't let you hurt
me.''

FOR ALL THE STRENGTH in her hands, for all the ath-
letic ability she showed in their daily jogs along the
beach, Taylor Angel was one hundred percent female, one hundred percent soft, gloriously rounded,
infinitely mysterious.

Her skin tasted of the same scented oils she used
during their massage sessions, smelling exotically of
sandalwood or some such perfume—Holden didn't
know which and didn't much care.

He could only concentrate on tasting her, sliding his
hands along her curves, feeling her respond beneath
his lips, his questing, slightly nervous fingers.

She gave him all of her and took back in equal
measure, her long legs wrapped tightly around his
back, holding him to her, giving herself up to him,
rocking with him in the ages-old rhythms of love-
making that somehow seemed so entirely new.

And when it was over, when they lay beside each
other on the bedspread there had been no time to turn
back, she curled into him like a sleepy kitten seeking
warmth—saying nothing, asking nothing. But purr-
ing contentedly.

While Holden lay there, stiff and tense, trying to
figure out what in hell had just happened to him.

''I should go upstairs,'' he said at last, the words
tearing a hole in his gut.

"I suppose so," Taylor answered, running her talented fingers down the middle of his chest, then lower. "Don't let me keep you."

"I've always thought physical therapists had to have a little of the sadist in them," Holden breathed, closing his eyes as her fingers sought him, found him—and reminded him that, although some of his fans might not share the opinion, he was still very much in his prime.

Growling deep in his throat, he rolled over onto his stomach, pinning Taylor beneath him. "I thought you said you'd never ask anything from me," he teased, even as he did a little "quarterback sneaking" of his own, gently pinching her nipples between thumb and forefinger as he rested his elbows on either side of her so she couldn't move away from him.

"Did I ask? I wasn't aware of having said a thing." Taylor's words seemed slightly slurred as she pushed her head back into the pillows, arching her neck. "Oh, that's so good. The things I could ask of you right now, Holden Masters. You just don't know!"

"Tell me," he whispered, his mouth taking the place of his fingers as he began laving her nipple, feeling it bloom beneath him like a rosebud opening to the sun. "Tell me, Taylor. Do you want me to do this?" He moved his hand between them, slid his fingers into her softness. "This? Maybe this?"

He sought her, found her, found the very center of her, and reveled in her immediate response. She lifted herself to him, ground herself against his hand even as he looked up at her face, saw how she had drawn her bottom lip between her teeth so she wouldn't give in, wouldn't ask for more. Not with words. But she was begging him soundlessly with her body, and he gave himself over to pleasuring her.

Never had he felt this deep desire to please. To go on pleasing. To find his own pleasure in that of his partner.

And when he felt her racking release, sensed her body going boneless beneath him, he slid into her, filling her, and felt her arms go around him, pulling his mouth down to hers so he could plumb her depths with his tongue, with all of him.

And when he left her in the last darkness before the dawn—still without more than a few words spoken between them—to go back to his own bed, he felt the first hurtful pangs of what it truly meant to be alone.

And when he took off his slacks and found the ring in his pocket, held it in his hand, then squeezed it inside his clenched fist, he felt more than alone.

But he didn't want to know why.

10

HOLDEN NOT ONLY "MASTERS" HIS
NEW "ANGEL" HAS PLAYED
byline Rich "The Nose" Newsome

Working with Nancy Marsh, sometime AP
reporter and a talented researcher who doesn't
just dig clams as she works the news along the
Jersey Shore, we have learned that Taylor Angel, Holden Masters's new squeeze, is not exactly an amateur when it comes to knowing her
way around the sports scene. Or, at the very
least, the locker room.

A bit of a "player" herself, the beauteous Ms.
Angel was, a few years back, briefly linked ro-
mantically with that superstud of the links,
Geoff Hamilton, runner-up in last year's Masters Tournament, and acknowledged international playboy bachelor.

Hamilton, when contacted after his disap-
pointing three-over-par round the first day of
play in the Hartford Open, refused to comment
on his association with Angel, except to say that
he could have used her that night because "she

gives a hell of a sweet back rub." When pressed, he added that he and Angel had been "just good friends."

Sound familiar, folks? Holden Masters has been "just good friends" with half the female population, and it appears Taylor Angel is no exception. Somebody must be rubbing somebody the right way, huh?

Wonder if she'll try baseball next and become a "three letter" sports groupie? Or is this really it, and has Masters been hooked, as his agent, Sidney Feldon, swears in near-constant press releases?

Or, if we dig a little deeper, is this whole thing nothing but a charade, and Holden Masters is really injured? His right cross sure leaves a lot to be desired.

And I oughta know.

Watch this space, sports fans, for further developments. And maybe let your wives take a peek at it now and then. This story seems to have something for everybody!

"WELL, AT LEAST he called you beauteous," Thelma Helper said, peering over Taylor's shoulder as the younger woman sat slumped at the dining room table, reading Rich "The Nose" Newsome's latest attempt at purple journalism.

"He also came within an inch of calling me a celebrity-hungry groupie. Know my way around a locker room, do I? And it sounds like he's onto us and has figured out that this is nothing but a sham engagement. Damn." Taylor laid the paper down, then covered Newsome's column with the style section. "I had to oversleep, didn't I? I suppose Holden has already seen this?" she asked the housekeeper.

"Missed a good breakfast up on the boardwalk, the two of you," Thelma said, picking up all of the newspaper, then wiping the tabletop with a damp cloth. "He started reading the newspaper before our coffee even came—and then hightailed it out of the restaurant, leaving me alone with that pair of young idiots. Woody emptied two full pitchers of syrup over his pancakes. Of course, he did eat blessed near a dozen of the things. Never does that with my pancakes!" She slapped the rag on the tabletop. "So, what are you going to do now?"

Taylor took a sip of hot coffee, then carefully replaced the cup in the saucer. "Do? Why should I *do* anything? You, of all people, shouldn't even ask me what I'm going to do. You know the engagement is all a cover-up, just a story Uncle Sid trumped up so nobody knows Holden was injured."

Thelma sniffed. "I also know how many beds I made up this morning. Now, you want to talk—or are you going to just sit there looking like Sam did when

I had to tell him I shrank his bowling shirt? Anyone would think you just lost your last friend."

Taylor looked at the older woman for a long moment, then dropped her head into her hands. "Oh, Thelma, I'm such a *jerk!*"

The housekeeper gave her a few solid thumps on the back—probably to reassure her, but with whacks strong enough to dislodge a Buick that might have gotten caught in her esophagus. "Stop feeling sorry for yourself. You're not a jerk, Taylor. With the track record Mr. Masters has in the romance department, he certainly can forgive you one puny little golf pro."

Still resting her forehead in her hands and trying to catch her breath, Taylor slowly twisted her head to the side to smile weakly up at the housekeeper. "You're such a comfort to me, Thelma," she said, then giggled in spite of herself.

"Thank you, child. That's what Sam always said," Thelma chirped as the timer went off, then went back into the kitchen to take a batch of Woody's favorite double-Dutch chocolate brownies out of the oven.

Taylor slumped back in the chair, spreading out her legs beneath the table as she rested her weight on her spine. "I'd better go call Uncle Sid," she reminded herself, grimacing. "He's going to want to know the whole story. And I don't even want to *think* about what I'm going to say to my parents. Thank God I told them all about that fiasco with Geoff when it happened."

"Talking to yourself?" Woody asked, sliding into the seat across from her, his hair still damp from his swim in the ocean and standing up all over his head as if he'd just gotten through toweling it. "Have you seen Holden? I want to ask him if I can invite this girl to dinner here tonight. Name's Tiffany, if you can believe it. Good kid, but sort of a nervous type, so I've got to be sure it's okay. You know, make sure the coast is clear before I bring her in here. Or haven't you read the paper yet?"

"I've read it, Woody," Taylor said dully, wishing Woody didn't look so damn young, so damn carefree. "Holden was pretty angry, huh?"

Woody reached up and began tugging on his earlobe. "Well... I don't like to say anything," he began slowly, "but you know how that one vein on his neck can sorta *stand out* when Tiff pulls one of her stupider stunts? Well... when he started reading The Nose's column—"

"Never mind, Woody," Taylor said, sighing. "I think I get the picture. Maybe I should just start packing. What do you think?"

"I think you don't know Holden," Woody responded, his tone suddenly cool, as if the blond beachboy with the toothpaste grin did, indeed, have a solemn side. A side that was somehow disappointed in his new friend, the woman he thought was going to marry his stepbrother. "I was talking about how mad Holden will be at The Nose, not you. Jeez,

Taylor, I thought you knew that. Well, see ya. I'm going back to the beach.''

Taylor waited until Woody was gone, and the sound of Thelma running water in the kitchen told her the woman was otherwise occupied, and then dragged herself down the half flight of stairs to the upper living room. She looked at the phone for a full minute, willing herself to pick it up, or willing Sidney Feldon to call her and put her out of her misery, then sat down at the table to work on the jigsaw puzzle she had begun the other day.

Could Woody be right? Could Holden's anger be directed against the reporter—and that miserable Nancy Marsh, who had certainly lived up to Holden's opinion of her—or was he angry with her?

He had every right to be. After all, she had given him no indication that she had ever been in the limelight before, or even within spitting distance of it—as she had been with Geoff Hamilton during the few months they'd been "an item."

To Holden, Taylor was just a simple girl—a working girl—a girl who still worried about what her parents might think of her—unexpectedly thrust as she was into the spotlight of his fame and not much liking it.

Which had been true enough once. She hadn't enjoyed being in public with Geoff when his fans recognized him. Probably because Geoff's way of dealing with his fans was either to snub them, insult them, or offer great, smacking kisses to the pretty women.

So unlike the way Holden dealt with his fans, which was up-front, congenial and understanding. In fact, everything about Geoff and Holden was different.

Geoff not only loved the spotlight, he craved it. When she got right down to it, really thought about it, *she* had been the Amanda Price of the moment in Geoff Hamilton's life. An attractive woman he could hang on his arm, make love to in his bed and then walk away from without a backward look when a younger, more attractive, gushing young idiot came along and threw herself at him.

But Taylor had *not* been another Amanda Price, which was probably why Geoff had dumped her. She had actually believed she loved Geoff Hamilton. Really, really loved him—so much so that she had fallen in bed with him without so much as a promise of love in return. Only after the fact had she thought to discuss marriage and babies and her idea of "happily ever after," stupidly believing that going to bed with a man and marriage to a man were like the chicken and the egg—it didn't much matter which came first as long as you could still make a good omelet.

Oh, yes, she'd thought she had loved Geoffrey Hamilton—before she had met Holden Masters and learned that true love is worlds apart from anything she had felt for the golf pro.

*And this time you can't even say you were naive—
you already knew the score. You were just plain
dumb*, she told herself. *You're building up a great
track record, Angel. In fact, maybe your next "letter" should be in track—somone like a long-distance
runner. At least maybe he'd stay the course for a
while.*

HOLDEN HAD WALKED the empty beach from Twenty-
fifth Street all the way down to Third and back again.
He had climbed to the boardwalk for blocks at a time
to stay clear of the beach-erosion teams building up
the beaches with sand dredged from the ocean floor—
and if anyone had called out his name, asked for his
autograph as he walked by, well, he simply hadn't
heard them.

He had been much too busy mentally beating himself up royally for the mistakes he'd been making
these past weeks, these past years—maybe even for
eleven long years, ever since he had signed his first
multimillion-dollar professional contract.

He never should have *met* Amanda Price, let alone
the dozens of other ambitious young women he'd
used, and been used by, this past decade and more.

He never should have gone along with Sid's stupid
plan to use the shoulder injury as a contract-fattening
device.

He never should have agreed to come to Ocean
City, to hide from the press; hide his injury and the

fact that he needed physical and massage therapy in order to regain full use of the injured muscles of his shoulder.

He shouldn't have opened his mouth to Amanda before thinking through the media stir his "engagement" to Taylor Angel would make of the whole affair.

He shouldn't have popped the widely acknowledged, vindictive Rich "The Nose" Newsome in the eye.

And mostly, he should never have taken Taylor Angel to bed!

"Bad mistake, Masters," he told himself for about the thousandth time as he opened the door to the condo at precisely 10:30 a.m. and stepped into the coolness of the ground-floor foyer. "Bad, bad mistake."

"Holden? Is that you?"

He turned to his right and saw Taylor standing in the living room cum workout center, busily wiping at the doughnut-shaped headrest with rubbing alcohol. She was dressed all in white this morning. A cropped sweater barely reached her waist, letting him see her flat stomach, the stretch of muscles in the small of her back as she put a prodigious amount of effort into the simple act of wiping the headrest.

Her shorts were very short. Cotton duck, he supposed the fashion designers called the heavy white fabric that, when she walked around the table, walked with her, became a part of her—and caused a lump to lodge in his throat that would probably remain there until the day he died and could no longer remember the sight of those damn, damn shorts.

And the legs under them.

And the honey blond hair knotted in a ponytail at her nape, the white terry-cloth sweatband encircling her smooth, golden tan forehead.

And the memory of her as she had been last night— warm and alive and perfect in every way.

"Yeah. Yeah, it's me," he forced out at last as he walked toward the living room the way a condemned man might drag his feet on his way to the gas chamber, realizing that it was time for his daily massage and cruelty-to-Holden session—one he'd rather forgo this morning. "You're ready for me?"

Dumb question, Masters, he berated himself, barely keeping from slapping himself on the forehead with the flat of his hand. *She's not ready for you. She's hating your guts, having given herself to you last night, only to find herself the butt of Rich Newsome's jokes in this morning's newspaper. She's about as ready for you as she is for another jellyfish on the beach. But she's a professional, and a responsible person, and she's going to keep doing her job, no matter how much she wants to cut and run.*

He stripped off his shirt as he crossed to the table, then lay down on the burgundy surface without looking at Taylor again. She had been getting more aggressive in her therapies—still taking about ten minutes to warm his muscles, make them easier to work with. But last week she had added even more deep muscle massage, mixed with some stretching and molding that had not yet ceased to surprise him with the occasional discovery of yet another sore spot, yet another small knot in the muscles he could have sworn were fully recovered.

He stared at the carpet—he was really beginning to harbor a lot of animosity over brown carpeting—then closed his eyes as her fingers first made contact with his back. Her fingers were cold, almost icy, although it was only comfortably cool in the condo, and her touch seemed more tentative than assured.

As if she was afraid.

As if she was nervous.

As if she was fighting a nearly uncontrollable urge to choke him?

"I'm sorry about that article."

He relaxed as he realized they had both said the same thing at the same time. "No fair, Taylor. This is my apology, not yours. Wait your turn."

She rushed into speech before he could say another word. "But I should have told you about Geoff. The moment you warned me that Nancy Marsh would find a way to get back at me after I did everything but tell her to take a hike. I was Geoff's therapist, and it certainly was no secret that we had been together. I should have realized that somebody would find out about Geoff, put two and two together and figure out that you really *are* injured. And relax, would you, please—I'm going to break my fingers trying to work your deltoid."

Holden dutifully concentrated on becoming as boneless as a jellyfish, Taylor's "magic" already beginning to ease some of the tension out of his shoulders, his upper back. "Geoff Hamilton was and is none of my business. And Rich Newsome is a damn lousy sports reporter and an even worse gossip columnist. Sid will handle him, handle all of it. But your name should never have shown up in that column. Your reputation should never have been a part of this whole mess. And I'm sorry for that, Taylor. Really, really sorry."

"And last night, Holden?" Taylor asked, moving to the head of the table in order to use her balled fists and the leverage of her body to "pull" some of the tension out of his neck. He lay very still, trying to remember to breathe, as her fists slowly moved up either side of his neck, pushing the tension higher into his skull, where it seemed to evaporate into the ether as she then ran her fingers in small circles behind his ears.

All his tension, the tension that knotted his back, tortured his mind, swiftly moved south to settle in his lower gut, in the immediate flare of the passion her question had jogged him into remembering. "You know what I think about last night, Taylor," he said,

ducking the question—and the completely unaccept-
able answer that had presented itself to him as he
walked along the boardwalk, watching young parents walking past him, pushing baby strollers, holding the hands of their toddlers. "We're two adults.
We knew what we were doing. And, even if I say so
myself, I think we did it pretty damn well.''

He glared down at the brown rug—listening to the
CD of Yanni's supposedly lulling instrumental music for a full five minutes after Taylor had raced out
of the living room, slamming the outside door of the
condo behind her—mentally beating himself up for
being a college-educated sports jock with all the finesse of a center trying to snap a greased pigskin on
a rain-muddy field.

11

THE NEXT THREE DAYS at the lime-sherbet condo would always remind Taylor of disjointed scenes from old Laurel and Hardy movies or snatches of Keystone Kops madness—even a bit of Three Stooges comedy.

Where Holden was, she wasn't.

Where she was, Holden avoided.

Where they both inevitably ended up—the dinner table, passing in the hallways—everyone else in the condo tried desperately *not* to be.

Woody ran facefirst into a corner of the archway in the kitchen in his laughable panic to make a fast getaway the night Taylor was buttering a piece of toast at the counter just as Holden exited the master suite to refill his soda glass.

Tiffany had taken to yelling up the staircase well, "Louise to Thelma—is the coast clear?" before she and Lance set foot beyond the ground-floor foyer.

And Thelma, being the epitome of grace and charm and tact that had become her hallmark, would then stick the little fingers of both hands into the sides of her mouth and whistle once for "all clear" and twice for "run for your life!"

It was ridiculous, really.

Really.

And almost funny.

Except that Taylor's heart was breaking.

She had given herself, completely and unreservedly, to a man who had told her up front that he was no more than a man with a need, a desire—and a firm grasp on his own independence.

She had entered into a sham engagement, then twisted the facts all around in her head until somewhere, deep down inside her, she had begun to *believe* Sid's press releases.

And that was dumb, really.

Really.

And not funny at all.

And Taylor's heart was *still* breaking.

"Stupid, stupid, *stupid!*" she muttered under her breath as she walked along the shore just as the sun was peeking above the horizon, turning the world golden—not that Taylor noticed the daily miracle she had anticipated with such awe no more than a few days ago. "And getting more stupid by the day. You have to get out of here, Taylor. Get out of here *now.*"

But Sid had phoned her from Maui, begged her to stay, and she had promised she would. For at least another two weeks, until Sid could complete the negotiations that were "going great guns now, honey."

Not that she was doing Holden or his rapidly recovering shoulder much good. He didn't show up for his massage sessions anymore. He ran on the beach at eight, a full two hours after her own solitary run. And he could do his simple physical therapy exercises himself.

She had become about as necessary to the career of the Master of the Game as fertilizer on artificial turf. "Bad analogy," she told herself, wincing, then smiled. "Although it sure does describe how I feel."

Hearing the sound of her name being called, Taylor looked to her left and stopped. She raised her eyebrows as Nancy Marsh hastily and quite clumsily made her way across the beach, her high heels sinking into the soft sand.

"Ms. Angel! May I have a word with you, please?" the reporter shouted, sending a pair of sea gulls screeching into the air. "Please?"

Taylor wasn't in the mood. "Should I turn my back first, Ms. Marsh, and give you a better target?" she asked, not liking the woman any better at the moment than she had the first time she'd met her.

Nancy stopped three feet away from Taylor, putting up a shaking hand to push her dark hair away from her face. "I deserved that, didn't I?" she asked, still trying to catch her breath, then bent down to take off her wet, sand-encrusted shoes. "You'd think, considering the fact that I do the 'Beach Beat,' I'd be smart enough to keep sneakers in my car, wouldn't you? I guess it's too late now to save these, though. I should have taken them off. That's me—do first, think later.''

Taylor felt her lips stretching in a small, commiserating smile. ''You're not the only one guilty of that particular failing these days, Nancy. There's no one around to see you. Do you want to slip off those panty hose, as well? I want to keep walking, if you don't mind. We can talk as we go.''

Nancy pulled a plastic bag out of her huge purse and dropped her shoes inside it, to be closely followed by her rolled-up panty hose. ''Okay, all set. But some ground rules first. You'll see that I have no steno pad, no pencils—and no miniature voice-activated tape recorder hidden in my purse. You can check if you want. I left all that in my car. I'm not a reporter today, Taylor. Just another woman. What we say to each other will be strictly personal and off-the-record. I promise. Just us two girls, talking.''

Taylor was becoming more than slightly intrigued. ''All right. Deal,'' she said, putting out her right hand, which Nancy accepted with a grateful thank-you.

Taylor then turned in the general direction of Atlantic City and began walking, Nancy at her side, the former in her pink spandex running outfit, the latter in a two-piece navy blue linen business suit and a white blouse with a pert Peter Pan collar. *The new*

Odd Couple, Taylor thought, feeling more relaxed by the moment.

After a few minutes spent talking about the weather, which was perfect, Taylor brought the subject around to Nancy's presence, which reminded her of just how *imperfect* her life was right now. "What is it you want to say anyway? If it has anything to do with how I can fill Rich Newsome's car with chocolate pudding and not get caught, well, I'm all ears."

"I'll supply the whipped cream," Nancy told her, bending to pick up a broken shell, then throwing it with enough force that, if Rich Newsome had been her target, he'd be running for his life. "He used me, you know. Used me, complimented me on my nose for news—that's what he called it—sent me digging, doing his dirty work for him, and then he scooped me. Oh, sure, he gave me credit in his column—the bastard—but he still scooped me. I couldn't sell my story to anyone after that. And I've got two kids to raise on my own. The louse! And I mean Newsome *and* my ex. Both louses."

"That's too bad," Taylor said, sure she was still missing something. Nancy Marsh hadn't come running after her to apologize for digging up the old news about Geoff. So far, she was only angry because Newsome had scooped her. If she expected Taylor to join in that particular pity party, well, not in this lifetime!

Nancy bobbed her head in agreement. "Yeah. And it was more than too bad. It stank big time. Look-it, Taylor, I'm not going to apologize for finding that stuff about you and the golf pro. I'm a reporter, and you're news. You became news the minute Holden Masters announced your engagement. Call it the price of fame, call it the press appealing to the lowest common denominator—doesn't matter what you call it. You're news. Holden Masters is news. His contract negotiations are news. His injury was news when it happened, and hiding from the press only made it worse. Do you understand what I'm saying?"

"Oh, yeah," Taylor answered. "I understand. Although it doesn't make any of this easier to swallow. You've got a rotten job, Nancy."

The reporter smiled. "No, I just got greedy. I have a great job, when you get right down to it. I live at the shore all year, reporting on all the hermit crab contests and sand-sculpting events. Good, family stuff. Lots of times I can take the kids with me on assignment. But news like Holden Masters doesn't drop into my lap very often. And, like I said, I got greedy—saw a way I could get my byline national. Only after I'd done it did I think about what sort of effect it might have on you. And for that, I do apologize. That, and the ear blistering I got from Holden Masters the day Newsome's column appeared."

"You want to run that last part by me one more time?" Taylor asked, looking at the reporter, who was shaking her head as if remembering something unpleasant. "Holden *called* you?"

"He sure did. And, believe me, you don't want to know *what* he called me!" She grinned. "No, that's not exactly true. He was a perfect gentleman, never even raised his voice. But I was in little bitty pieces by the time he was done with me. He told me all about you, how sweet you are, how unaffected you are by his fame, his money. He told me how he nearly had to get down on his hands and knees and *beg* you to accept the ring, and how lucky he was to have found you. Where is it anyway? The ring, I mean. Never mind. I guess you're afraid of losing it on the beach. Don't blame you. I heard from the friend of a friend of a friend that the thing cost a small fortune. And *that* I didn't print! I've learned my lesson. I'm sticking to covering Fourth of July parades from now on. They're safer. But, boy, I had to tell you. That I'm sorry—and that I wish I had someone who loved me as much as Holden Masters loves you. You're a lucky, lucky girl."

Taylor looked straight into the rapidly rising sun, hoping her sudden tears would be blamed on its stunning brightness. "Yeah, Nancy. That's me. A lucky, lucky girl. So—you want to go up on the boardwalk and get a bag of freshly made chocolate-covered doughnuts? Suddenly I'm in the mood to eat something comforting and sinfully fattening."

HOLDEN PUT DOWN the free-weight as Woody and Tiffany knocked on the door to his room, then entered without waiting for permission. "What's up, guys?" he asked as they crossed to the king-size bed and sat down, staring at him as if they wanted to bore a hole straight through him. "And if you're thinking about another trip to Atlantic City, you can just forget it. I don't care if Thelma said she'd chaperon—especially since she found out about Tiffany's, um, *talent*. I'd as soon trust the three of you riding bareback on a Brahman bull in the middle of a china shop."

"Oh, you're *so* funny, Holden," Tiffany said, sniffing, which was pretty hard to do, seeing as how she had curled her upper lip in obvious disdain for her stepbrother. "Woody—isn't Holden funny? Ha. Ha. *Ha!*"

"Yeah, Tiff, he's a laugh riot," Woody answered, in agreement with his half sister for perhaps the second time in their lives.

Which might have been why Holden pulled himself far enough out of the doldrums he had been enjoying wallowing in to notice for the first time that Tiffany's hair was blond. And not orangey blond, or glows-in-the-dark blond. Just blond. Naturally blond. The way he remembered it being yesterday, when she was only a child asking to be taken for a piggyback ride down the curving stairs of Peter LeGrand's mansion.

"You look nice, Tiff," he said, smiling at her. "Really nice. I like your hair. And your outfit." The girl was wearing simple denim shorts and a red-and-white polka-dot tank top. She looked, well, *normal.*

Tiffany's mouth worked again, then her lips spread in a smile as she reached up a hand to touch her hair. "You really like it? Lance does, too, if you can believe that. Seeing as how I'm starting college in the fall, Taylor mentioned that I might want to get my act together a little better. You know, put on my college hat? Or should I say—my college *hair?* I really like Taylor, Holden. Maw-maw wouldn't care if I shaved my head. As a matter of fact, I think she did shave half of hers last year."

"Uh-huh," Holden responded absently, now taking a closer look at Woody, who looked much the same as he had these past years—very much like every other young Malibu surfer—and tried to see if there was anything different about him. There wasn't. It was the same old Woody. But then, he'd barely gotten used to the idea that "the same old Woody" had just been accepted into graduate school. "Woody? You're looking serious. Is there a problem?"

"I don't know. You tell us, bro."

Holden picked up the free-weight again and began doing arm curls, avoiding Woody's suddenly piercing eyes. "What are you talking about?" he asked, instantly regretting the approach he had chosen. His stepsiblings might be young, but they were far from dumb.

"Oh—*duh,* Woody! What are we talking about?" Tiffany exploded dramatically and rather sarcastically. "Gee, Woody, do you suppose we're wrong? Do you suppose Holden here isn't screwing up the best thing that ever happened to him? Do you suppose we, like, haven't *noticed* what's going on around here?"

"All right, all right!" Holden apologized hastily. "I get the point. You've obviously noticed that Taylor and I aren't exactly speaking to each other right now." They remained silent and staring. "Okay, so we're definitely not speaking to each other right now. But she's still here, isn't she?"

"Only to keep up her end of the bargain," Tiffany retorted, then ducked as Woody took a halfhearted swing at her. "Oops, I wasn't supposed to say that, was I?"

Woody got up from the bed and began to pace, looking much older than his years. "Look, Holden, Thelma told us all about it. How you and your agent talked Taylor into pretending to be your fiancée so you could hide your injury until it was all healed and Sid could get you a better deal on your new contract."

"And so he could get rid of Amanda, Woody," Tiffany volunteered. "Don't forget that part. After all, that's what started all of this in the first place."

"Right, Tiff. Can't forget Amanda. Anyway, Holden, I can understand that Taylor's ticked off over that story about her and that golf pro, but don't you think you could just apologize and get it over with? Because of that stupid article? And if you'd only *talk* to each other, well, this whole mess would work out."

"You think so, do you, Woody?" Holden did another arm curl, then set the weight on the floor.

'Yeah. Yeah, I do. You see," he went on, perching himself on the edge of the bed again, "I had a little talk with Taylor the day Newsome's column came out, and I think *she* thinks you're mad at her over the story, and not the other way around. But if you never even *talk* to each other about who is mad at who and why, well, then Tiff and I are just maybe going to have to go on back to California and not stay here and watch while you ruin your life the way Peter does every other year. Does that make sense?"

"We like Taylor, Holden," Tiffany added when Woody stopped speaking. "We really, really like her."

"And we really, really think you're being a first-class chump," Thelma chimed in from the doorway. "Now, if that's settled, who wants to go to Cape May for a little shopping and some dinner? Woody, Tiffany? I think we should be making ourselves scarce around here tonight—give Holden some room to maneuver, you know? Tiffany—there's one of those new-age-y type crystal shops you'd really like and,

Woody, I'll show you how to get to the zoo. If they don't keep you and put you in a cage with the rest of the wild animals, we can even drive down to the end of the highway after dinner and watch the sun set over the bay. You'll think you're back in California.''

"Wow, Thelma! Kewl! I'll go call Lance!'' Tiffany was already heading for the door.

"Tiff—'' Holden called after her, then shook his head. "Oh, what's the use? Go ahead, Woody. Have a good time.''

"And you'll talk to Taylor?''

"Don't push, Woody.''

"Well, will you?'' Thelma demanded. "Or are you going to let that woman go? You know, sometimes you have to tell a man what he's thinking before he knows he's thinking it himself. Why, I remember the time Sam—''

"Thelma,'' Holden began warningly, then grinned. "All right, all right, I'll *talk* to her. But are you two sure you don't want to take over Sid's role in my contract negotiations? I think you've both missed your calling. You're very persuasive, in a cheerfully abrasive sort of way.''

Thelma stuck a cigarette in her mouth and lit it. "Just make an honest woman of her, that's all I'm asking. And feed her—that always works. I've got two steaks marinating in the fridge, and you can put a couple of potatoes on the grill to bake—and slice up some of those ripe New Jersey tomatoes I've got sitting on the windowsill. Oh, and I wouldn't mind a move to Philadelphia, in case you were wondering. Always did like those hot dogs they serve at the stadium. Think about it. You two are going to need a housekeeper, you know. Especially when the babies start coming.''

"I'll certainly keep your offer in mind, Thelma," Holden responded, trying to keep a straight face.

"Do that," she answered, then reached into the pocket of her apron and pulled out Taylor's ring, tossing it to him so quickly he reached up and caught it in self-defense. "I'd even give up smoking for the babies, which Sam was always after me to do anyway. Now, give that sparkler back to her, and this time make sure she knows why she's getting it. Come on, kid, let's get this show on the road.''

Woody put his arm around the little woman and they walked out of the room.

"So, I think that went well," Holden heard Thelma say to Woody in obvious satisfaction as they headed toward the staircase.

Woody just turned his head to look at Holden, and grinned.

12

HOLDEN WAS WHISTLING as he scrubbed potato skins, thinking how great Thelma was and how he could see her in his life—in his and Taylor's life. In the house they'd buy on the outskirts of Philadelphia. Well, not in the house, maybe. But in one of those carriage-house apartments that big, rambling old houses seemed to have. Yeah, that would do it. Close, but not too close.

And it would have to be a really big house. With room for Woody and Tiffany when they wanted to come East and visit him and Taylor and the kids. With lots of land around it, too, for horses, maybe?

It just kept getting better and better, this rosy future Holden was building as he scrubbed potatoes— until he noticed with surprise that he had washed six of the things. Who did he think he was feeding—an army?

This was going to be good. Really good. Thelma had set the table in the upstairs living room before she left, right down to the candles she'd placed in holders she'd dug up somewhere. The champagne was on ice. The steaks were still marinating. The tomatoes were sliced, arranged on a plate and cooling in the refrigerator. The potatoes were ready for the grill.

And for dessert? Ah...dessert!

Holden grinned.

He knew it was a grin—much more than a smile.

And he knew he probably looked stupid.

And he didn't care.

"'Just get me to the church on time!'" he sang as he patted the pocket of his team shorts, feeling the ring that resided there. This was going to work. Oh, yes, it was. A little groveling, a little apologizing—maybe some hangdog looks—and then the ring. This time, for *real*.

And finally, dessert.

He grinned again.

And then the doorbell rang, and he frowned. The doorbell wasn't supposed to ring. Taylor had a key, so she couldn't be ringing it. So who was ringing it? Some reporter? A neighbor asking for an autograph?

Whoever, it is, he told himself as he stepped out onto the small porch and quickly tossed two potatoes into the already-heated propane grill, then raced down the stairs two at a time, they were going to be on their way in two seconds flat, because Taylor would be back from her late-afternoon run on the beach any minute, and the last thing he wanted was any sort of interruption.

It was going to be hard enough to make her stand still and listen to him as he groveled, told her what a jerk he'd been and how much he loved her, really loved her, without having an audience around!

"What?" he barked out as he threw open the door, then pushed his head forward as if he needed a closer look to recognize the man standing there in a wild pink-and-green flowered shirt and baggy shorts that revealed his knobby knees. There was a lei of rather crushed and wilted orchids around his neck. *"Sid?"*

He stepped back two paces, not knowing whether to be shocked, angry or amused, and watched as the much shorter man walked into the foyer, then repeated, *"Sidney? Is that you?"*

"Uncle Sidney?" Taylor exclaimed from the doorway—obviously back from her run—then ran inside to fall into the agent's open arms and give him a huge hug.

"Here's my girl!" her uncle crowed, returning her embrace. "Taylor, Taylor, my multi-multi-unbelievably-*multi*million-dollar stroke of genius!" He held her at arm's length. "Let me look at you. You've been wonderful, wonderful!"

"You look wonderful, Uncle Sidney!" Taylor answered, still avoiding Holden's gaze.

"He looks like he was caught in a freak flower-shop explosion," Holden grumbled as Sid took the orchid lei from his neck and placed it around Taylor's, then stood on tiptoe to kiss her on both cheeks. "They let you on an airplane dressed like that? Isn't there some sort of dress code? You know—nothing that might frighten small children?"

Sidney, never one to stand on ceremony—or be easily insulted—headed for the stairs, Taylor's hand still in his. "It was a long, long flight, with two layovers I don't even want to remember, let alone talk about right now. I need a drink, Holden," he said, hesitating on the first landing for a moment, then unerringly heading for the next level and the carefully set table and the bottle of champagne that sat in a plastic ice bucket on the coffee table.

He pulled the bottle from its icy cocoon and looked around for a corkscrew, which he spied not far from the bucket. "One thing I have to say about you, Holden. You sure do know how to live. And so do I, seeing as how I'm the one who lined all this up for you. Nice place, and that housekeeper I hired must be a treasure, setting you up like this every night. Now, go get another glass, and we'll toast your new contract."

"The negotiations are over?" Taylor asked, her voice quiet, her smile replaced by a closed, shuttered look that revealed more than it hid. Holden would have been cheered by her sudden sadness if he didn't believe his groveling was going to have to be done while Taylor was madly throwing clothing in a suitcase in anticipation of running away from him.

"Over? Honey, it's just the beginning!" Sidney crowed, puffing out his chest. "Everything we wanted, Holden. Just the way I said it would happen when I talked you into this in the first place. *Everything!* And a couple of things I didn't even think to ask for—if you can believe that. And all because of Rich Newsome. That right cross of yours put the seal on it. If you can punch out a creep, you can throw a ball—or words to that effect. That's what the owners said, anyway. They can't wait for you to come back to the city and sign on the dotted line so all the other teams will go away. Which we'll do, right? Tonight okay with you? Holden, for the next five years—five years!—you are safely set in Philadelphia."

The cork slipped out of the bottle with a small *pop,* and Sidney wrinkled his nose in pleasure like some psychedelic pixie.

"So? Holden? And you'd be waiting for—what? It's okay. You can bow down and worship at my feet now."

"Huh? Oh, yeah—thanks, Sid," Holden said as Taylor slowly walked from the room, heading for the stairs. "Now do me a favor, Sid, okay?"

"Anything, Holden," his agent agreed happily. "Just name it."

"Go away, Sid," Holden said, following Taylor. "I'll call you tomorrow. But for now—there's a bonus in it for you if you'll just go far, far away."

WELL, THAT'S THAT, Taylor thought as she walked down the hallway to her bedroom, wishing she didn't have to blink quite so much to keep the tears at bay. *As the superheroes say before flying off, "I'll be on my way now. My work here is done!"*

She strode into the room, leaving the door open behind her, dragged her large duffel bags out of the closet and threw them onto the bed, then walked over to the dresser and opened the top drawer.

"Going somewhere?"

Taylor bit her bottom lip as she looked into the mirror on the wall over the dresser and saw Holden's reflection in the glass. "Aren't you? Uncle Sidney said he wanted you to drive back to Philadelphia with him tonight. There's a limousine waiting outside, you know. I saw it when I got back from the beach."

A door closed somewhere in the distance. "The sound you just heard was our Don Ho impersonator heading back to New York," Holden said. He walked into the room to stand behind Taylor, then reached around her to push the drawer shut, leaving his hands pressed on top of the dresser. "I'm not going anywhere."

If she turned around, just moved her feet a little and turned, she'd be in his arms. Face-to-face. Heartbeat to heartbeat. She remained where she was, closing her eyes so she didn't have to look at his reflection. "You turned down the contract? Uncle Sidney seemed to think it was a great deal. Well, either way, I don't see as how it's any of my business. We haven't even *talked* to each other in three days, for crying out loud."

Without a word, Holden pushed himself away from the dresser and moved to the doorway once more—leaving, she was sure. *Sure, Angel, remind him that he's mad at you. Good job!* She let out a shaky breath, part of her wanting him gone, the other part of her wanting to scream at him to stay.

But he didn't go anywhere. He just stood in the doorway, looking into the mirror, silently daring her to turn around.

"What?" she exclaimed at last, as her nerves, already stretched taut, snapped. "What do you want? A farewell massage? Well, you can just forget it, buster."

"I was hoping we could have dinner," he said, sounding as innocent as a choirboy—which was her first clue that *something* was very, very wrong. Or very, very right? "But I suppose a massage wouldn't hurt. Come with me?"

"I'd sooner go wading in a snake pit," she told him, pressing back against the dresser as if the piece of furniture could offer her some sort of protection from her own raging emotions that told her half a loaf was reported to be better than one. Would it really be so bad to be in his arms again just one more time? "And where is everybody anyway?" she asked, searching for something to say that wouldn't end up with her telling him exactly what was on her mind. "And who set that table upstairs in the living room? We've never done that before."

Holden leaned his tall frame against the doorjamb and rubbed a hand across his mouth—still looking for that nonexistent mustache, Taylor supposed. It was one of his most endearing habits, not that she had noticed. Or kept a mental record of every sweet, endearing thing the man did. She rolled her eyes, calling herself every kind of fool she could imagine.

"What was that for?" Holden asked, obviously referring to her expression. "Or did you just figure out that you and I are alone here in the condo? Did it finally occur to you that Tiffany and Woody and Thelma are gone, and that the table upstairs is set for two, and that, since Sid came and fouled up my plans, I'm going back ten to punt, trying my damnedest to figure out a way to tell you what a jerk I've been?"

Taylor stuck out her tongue to wet her suddenly dry lips. "You've been a what?"

He pushed himself away from the door, made his way back down the hallway, then turned up the stairs.

She followed, of course. He must have known she'd follow him. How many times did someone get to hear the Master of the Game call himself a jerk?

"I said," he continued once they were both back in the upper living room and he had handed her a flute of champagne, "I'm a jerk. I've been a jerk for so long that it took me a while to figure out just how much of a jerk I've been—but I think I'm getting the hang of it now. Want to hear me say it again? I'm a jerk, I'm a jerk, I'm a damn jerk!"

Taylor giggled in spite of herself, then took a sip of champagne.

"Hey—you can stop me anytime, you know," Holden complained, taking the glass from her hand and placing it on the coffee table. "Humble has never been my most successful play."

"But you do humble very well, Holden," she told him. She walked over to the table, picked up the book of matches left there so that she could light the candles. "So, are we having crow for dinner? I could use a serving or two myself."

"What do *you* have to apologize about?" he asked, and she turned to him and smiled, for he really, really was a wonderfully handsome, appealing man.

And she loved him, so even his clumsy attempts at thanking her for her help before saying goodbye seemed somehow special in her eyes, in her breaking heart.

"Well, according to Woody—nothing," she began, no longer able to meet Holden's eyes. "I thought you'd be angry with me because of that newspaper article—because of Geoff—but Woody assured me you wouldn't be. So," she said, then hesitated. She cleared her throat. "So I guess I'm apologizing for thinking I should apologize. And for not being quite the sophisticated woman of the world I let you think I was."

He took three small steps in her direction. "Meaning?" he prompted.

"Mean-ing," she pronounced carefully, finding she had to clear her throat again, "that I'm not real adult about...about...um..."

"Going to bed with a man and then saying thanks, it's been fun?" Holden supplied, and Taylor didn't know whether to kiss him or slug him in the jaw.

"Yeah. That," she said gruffly.

"Going to bed with a man who is well known for his affairs, his total lack of commitment?"

"That, too."

"A man who never said a word about love, or marriage, or even if he would be around in the morning?"

"All right, all right! *Yes!* There's no reason to draw blueprints on this, is there? I think we both get the point. Can I slink away now?" She looked past him, up the half flight of stairs and to the sliding doors that looked out over the small landing leading to the roof. "Holden? Is the condo on fire?"

"On fire?" He looked at her dumbly for a moment, then whirled around to run up the stairs three at a time. "My *potatoes!*"

Potatoes? she mouthed silently, watching him tear up the stairs and out to the smoking grill. She could have gone then. Could have tiptoed back down the stairs—or hopped down them carrying lead weights to make more noise, because Holden was already long gone and wouldn't hear her. But she couldn't help herself. The look of comic dismay on the man's face had her melting all over, full of love for him now as she would always be—and *liking* him so damn much that she was nearly bursting with it.

She followed him up the stairs, stopping off in the kitchen for the tongs Thelma kept in the drawer next to the sink. "Here," she said moments later, holding the utensil out to Holden, who had lifted the cover of the grill and was now trying to fan away the smoke with his hand. "Try taking the potatoes off the grill and putting them in that sand bucket."

"Thanks," he said, his cheeks running with tears from all the smoke. "Damn it, Taylor, would you look what you've reduced me to?"

"Crying?" she teased, beginning to think she might just have lost her mind.

"No, damn it—*cooking!*" He dropped the charred potatoes into the sand bucket and pushed her back inside the condo, sliding the door closed on the worst of the smoke. "I'm going to kill Thelma when she gets home. Her and her bright ideas!"

"It's the soap opera," Taylor supplied helpfully. "Thelma's a born romantic, you know."

"She's a born meddler, and so are Tiffany and Woody." And then he smiled, putting out his hand and running his fingertip down Taylor's cheek. "I don't know what I'd do without them. Or without you. Taylor—"

She backed away from him, holding out her hands as if to ward him off. "No, Holden," she said firmly. "I'm not doing this again. We're attracted to each other. We have been from the first—as you've already said, and as I've agreed. We went to bed together. But that's it. Call it a mistake, call it a one-night stand, or call it two adults who knew what they were doing and did it very well. Isn't that what you said? But don't ask me to do it again. I'm just not strong enough."

His grin was wicked, more than wicked. "You want a celibate marriage?" he asked, reaching into the pocket of his shorts and pulling out the ring she had hidden so well between her mattress and box spring.

Thelma! Taylor thought before she couldn't think at all, because Holden Masters was down on one knee in front of her—his clothes and face smudged with smoke, his hair falling into his eyes—and he was saying something that sounded an awful lot like, "I love you, Taylor. Please marry me."

Epilogue

MASTERS NUPTIALS STUN MORNING JOGGERS
byline Nancy Marsh

OCEAN CITY, NEW JERSEY (AP)—

With early-morning joggers, circling sea gulls and a few excited tourists also present, this family resort town was the scene yesterday as Taylor Angel, professional physical therapist, and Holden Masters, All-Pro quarterback, said their vows on the beach in an intimate, surprise dawn ceremony.

The bride was ethereally beautiful in an off-the-shoulder, ivory silk gown as she was escorted over a long sea green carpet that led to the shore, attended by the groom's stepsister, Tiffany LeGrand, and her matron of honor, Thelma Helper.

Masters, resplendent in a custom-fitted tuxedo, awaited his bride at the water's edge, his stepbrother, Woodstock LeGrand, serving as best man.

Other than the bride's parents, Edward and Mary Angel, and Masters's agent, Sidney Feldon, this reporter was the only invited guest at the ceremony, and the happy couple will be granting me an exclusive interview upon their return from their honeymoon hideaway.

Masters, now the highest-paid player in the history of the National Football League, will report to training camp as planned, August 1.

"SHE REALLY LAID IT on with a trowel, didn't she?" Holden remarked as he listened to his bride of a little more than twenty-four hours read the story in the newspaper that had come up to their suite at the Taj Mahal on their breakfast tray. "The Nose must be kicking himself up and down Broad Street, knowing he's been scooped by a local reporter. God, but that makes my day!"

"And it's not a bad picture of all of us, even if Sid was yelling about getting sand in his new Gucci loafers. Besides, I thought *I* had made your day," Taylor teased, putting down the newspaper and climbing back into bed beside her husband. "At least, I believe that's what you said no more than an hour ago. I distinctly remember you lying there—breathing rather heavily for such a seasoned athlete—and saying, 'Taylor, you've—'"

Holden pulled her against him, kissing her forehead. "You know what I mean. Love me as much as I love you, Mrs. Masters?"

"I *adore* you, Mr. Masters," she answered, laying her head against his shoulder. "I'd adore you if you were flat broke—although that doesn't mean I'm going to ask you to turn down that new contract. I'm no dope, you know. But you're still not getting a massage. Not until after we take a run on the beach."

"You're a hard woman, Taylor Masters," Holden groused, pushing himself up and away from her, climbing out of the bed and stretching his arms over his head as he pretended to walk toward the bathroom.

She had just snuggled down against the mound of pillows, smiling in obvious satisfaction, when he turned and swooped onto the bed, taking her into his arms and kissing her until she had to pull away to catch her breath.

Taylor wriggled slightly beneath him, doing things to his insides he hadn't believed possible. "Something tells me we're not jogging this morning, are we?" she asked, lifting her head to nibble at his earlobe.

Holden grinned down at her. "Darling—exercise is exercise."

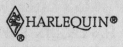

Not The Same Old Story!

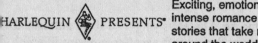 Exciting, emotionally intense romance stories that take readers around the world.

 Vibrant stories of captivating women and irresistible men experiencing the magic of falling in love!

 Bold and adventurous— Temptation is strong women, bad boys, great sex!

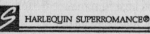 Provocative, passionate, contemporary stories that celebrate life and love.

 Romantic adventure where anything is possible and where dreams come true.

 Heart-stopping, suspenseful adventures that combine the best of romance and mystery.

LOVE & LAUGHTER Entertaining and fun, humorous and romantic—stories that capture the lighter side of love.

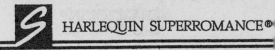

LOOK FOR OUR FOUR FABULOUS MEN!

Each month some of today's bestselling authors bring
four new fabulous men to Harlequin American Romance.
Whether they're rebel ranchers, millionaire power brokers
or sexy single dads, they're all gallant princes—and
they're all ready to sweep you into lighthearted fantasies
and contemporary fairy tales where anything is possible
and where all your dreams come true!

You don't even have to make a wish...Harlequin American
Romance will grant your every desire!

Look for Harlequin American Romance wherever Harlequin
books are sold!

HARLEQUIN®

I N T R I G U E®

THAT'S INTRIGUE—DYNAMIC ROMANCE AT ITS BEST!

Harlequin Intrigue is now bringing you more—more men and mystery, more desire and danger. If you've been looking for thrilling tales of contemporary passion and sensuous love stories with taut, edge-of-the-seat suspense—then you'll *love* Harlequin Intrigue!

Every month, you'll meet four new heroes who are guaranteed to make your spine tingle and your pulse pound. With them you'll enter into the exciting world of Harlequin Intrigue—where your life is on the line and so is your heart!

Harlequin Intrigue—we'll leave you breathless!

Harlequin®
Historical

If you're a serious fan of historical romance,
then you're in luck!

Harlequin Historicals brings you
stories by bestselling authors, rising new stars
and talented first-timers.

Ruth Langan & Theresa Michaels
Mary McBride & Cheryl St.John
Margaret Moore & Merline Lovelace
Julie Tetel & Nina Beaumont
Susan Amarillas & Ana Seymour
Deborah Simmons & Linda Castle
Cassandra Austin & Emily French
Miranda Jarrett & Suzanne Barclay
DeLoras Scott & Laurie Grant…

You'll never run out of favorites.

Harlequin Historicals…they're too good to miss!

HARLEQUIN PRESENTS®

HARLEQUIN PRESENTS
men you won't be able to resist falling in love with...

HARLEQUIN PRESENTS
women who have feelings just like your own...

HARLEQUIN PRESENTS
powerful passion in exotic international settings...

HARLEQUIN PRESENTS
intense, dramatic stories that will keep you turning
to the very last page...

HARLEQUIN PRESENTS
The world's bestselling romance series!

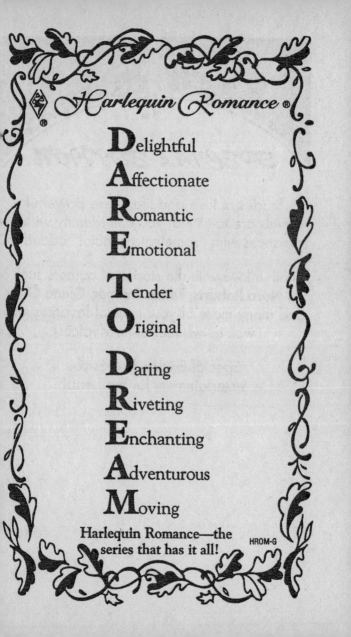

Harlequin Romance ®

Delightful

Affectionate

Romantic

Emotional

Tender

Original

Daring

Riveting

Enchanting

Adventurous

Moving

Harlequin Romance—the
series that has it all!

HROM-G

SPECIAL EDITION

Stories of love and life, these powerful
novels are tales that you can identify with—
romances with "something special" added in!

Fall in love with the stories of authors such
as **Nora Roberts, Diana Palmer, Ginna Gray**
and many more of your special favorites—as
well as wonderful new voices!

Special Edition brings you
entertainment for the heart!